THE SEVENTH SINNER

**Center Point
Large Print**

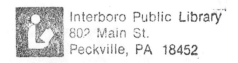

**This Large Print Book carries the
Seal of Approval of N.A.V.H.**

ॐ श्री गणेशाय नमः

ELIZABETH PETERS

THE SEVENTH SINNER

CENTER POINT PUBLISHING
THORNDIKE, MAINE • USA

BOLINDA PUBLISHING
MELBOURNE • AUSTRALIA

This Center Point Large Print edition
is published in the year 2002 by arrangement with
The Dominick Abel Literary Agency, Inc.

This Bolinda Large Print edition
is published in the year 2002 by arrangement with
David Grossman Literary Agency Ltd.

The text of this Large Print edition is unabridged.
In other aspects, this book may vary from the original
edition. Printed in Thailand. Set in 16-point
Times New Roman type by Bill Coskrey.

US ISBN 1-58547-188-7
BC ISBN 1-74030-996-0

US Cataloging-in-Publication data is available from the Library of Congress.

Australian Cataloguing-in-Publication is available from the Australian National Library.

British Cataloguing-in-Publication is available from the British Library.

ONE

JEAN would never forget her first encounter with Jacqueline Kirby. It was years before she could think about it without blushing all over. An acquaintance which begins with assault and battery, however inadvertent, can hardly be termed auspicious.

There was some slight excuse for Jean's behavior. All morning she had been working, or trying to work, in the Institute library. There were distractions. First and omnipresent was the siren call of the city outside the dusty library stacks. April in Paris is famous, but May in Rome has an allure that can distract the soberest student. The city of Michelangelo and the *dolce vita,* the capital of the papacy and the Caesars—whatever it is you may be seeking, you can find it somewhere in Rome. Jean's prized fellowship at one of the world's most famous institutions of art and archaeology was a poor substitute for Rome on a spring morning; and the call of duty was not as effective as Ulysses' waxen earplugs against the siren's song.

Michael was a second distraction, and if he was not as overwhelming as an entire city, he was closer at hand. Michael should have been working too; but his sense of duty was as neglected as his shaggy, shoulder-length brown hair. He dithered aimlessly about the stacks, peering at Jean through gaps in the shelved books and edging up to her whenever she got into a dark corner.

Emerging, breathless and disheveled, from one of these encounters, Jean had to admit she wasn't avoiding them as wholeheartedly as she might have done. Michael would leave her in peace if she retired into her office and closed the door. The small windowless cubicles assigned to the student fellows were Spartan affairs, with only a desk and chair and a couple of bookcases. The doors had glass panels on the upper halves, but they served the same purpose as the sported oak of Oxford. When the door was closed, the occupant did not wish to be disturbed. Nothing less than a fire or general insurrection justified so much as a knock.

As she stood contemplating her own office door, Michael caught up with her again. His arm went around her and Jean came back to her senses with a start to find that her undisciplined body was responding. She pulled away. All she needed was to be caught in dalliance by one of the members of the fellowship committee, two weeks before that committee met to decide on the renewal of student grants for a second year.

"All right," she hissed irritably. "I give up. . . . No, damn it, I don't mean that! I mean, let's get out of here."

Jean was never quite sure which of them was responsible for the disaster. The Institute's halls were magnificent expanses of polished marble. As Jean emerged from the library she saw that the corridor was deserted—a long, snowy stretch of emptiness, shining like ice and just as slippery. She couldn't resist. She broke into a run, with Michael in enthusiastic pursuit.

They turned the corner together. Jean had one flashing glimpse of a face, openmouthed in consternation, and then there was a melee of flailing arms and legs, a stifled shriek, and a dull thud. She and Michael, who had somehow kept their feet, stood staring down at a prostrate, motionless form.

"Holy Christ," said Michael sincerely. "Is she dead?"

The fallen woman didn't look very lively. Jean had seen her in the library during the past few weeks and had classified her, disinterestedly, as a summer visitor—a teacher or scholar. She usually wore neat tailored dresses and horn-rimmed glasses, and her hair was pulled back into a severe knot at the back of her neck.

In her present state of collapse she looked quite different. A huge purse had gone flying at the impact, and its contents littered the floor for yards around, like the debris left by a miniature tornado. The demure knee-length skirt had been disarranged, displaying legs that drew an admiring whistle from Michael. A shaft of sunlight fell across the woman's head and shoulders, spotlighting a face whose features looked pallid and austere—high cheekbones, a firm chin, long, curved lips like the mouth of an archaic Greek statue. The hair was spectacular. It had been loosened by the fall, and lay about the peaceful face like a pool of molten bronze, gleaming with amber highlights.

"Did we kill her?" Michael demanded.

"Don't be ridiculous. . . . I hope not!"

Suddenly, without preliminary fluttering or blinking, the closed eyes opened. They were a true, clear green, an unusual color for human eyes. They looked translucent, like seawater, and they focused on Jean with an expression of concentrated malevolence made all the more alarming by contrast with the placidity of the face in which they were set.

The woman's compressed lips parted.

"Here, too, O Lord?" a plaintive voice inquired.

Jean, who had been thinking in terms of concussion, revised her diagnosis. Clearly there was some kind of brain damage. She dropped to her knees.

"Don't try to talk," she said agitatedly. "Just don't move. Did you break anything? Did you—"

"Did *I* break anything?" The implacable green eyes moved on to examine Michael, who stirred uneasily. "I have no intention of moving. I may stay here for the rest of the day. It seems to be the safest place. Unless you trample on helpless bodies around here."

Jean sat back on her heels.

"I think you're all right."

"I am all right. Not good, but all right. No worse than usual . . . I talk like this all the time. Who are you?"

"Jean Suttman, Michael Casey," said Michael. "Do you want me to help you up?"

"*No,*" said his victim distinctly.

Michael sat down on the floor. "Who are you?" he asked conversationally.

"Jacqueline Kirby."

"Hello."

"Hello."

Jean looked from Michael, cross-legged on the floor like an Indian mystic, to Jacqueline, still prone and looking as if she had every intention of remaining in that position indefinitely. She began to laugh. The others contemplated her with disfavor, and their sour expressions only made her laugh harder. When she had calmed her-self, Jacqueline said severely, "If you have *quite* finished, you might start collecting my belongings."

"Sure," Jean said. She added meekly, "Would you mind getting up, Miss—Mrs.—Doctor—"

"Considering the informality of this meeting, you may call me Jacqueline. Why do you want me to get up? I'm perfectly comfortable."

"She doesn't care how you feel," Michael explained calmly. "She just wants to get the evidence of her crime up off the floor before one of the senior fellows comes along. They're meeting pretty soon to decide which of us gets a second year here."

"Oh, really," Jacqueline said thoughtfully.

Jean stopped in her crawling pursuit of compacts, pens, postcards, and a small bottle of what appeared to be crème de menthe.

"That 'really' has a blackmailing sound to it," she said. "You wouldn't. . . . Would you?"

"I guess not," Jacqueline said with regret. "Ah, well. You may help me up, Michael."

Michael obliged, with a last appreciative look at Jacque-line's knees. Jacqueline saw the look; stepping gently away from Michael, who was brushing haphazardly at her back, she remarked,

"Thank you. For everything . . . Show's over. I now revert to my real self."

She gathered in the fiery hair rippling down her back and began to knot it up.

"What are you doing that for?" Michael demanded. "Let it hang out and down and all like that. You have beautiful hair, lady."

"I know," Jacqueline said coolly. "It's my sole vanity, however, and it doesn't suit my present image. Jean, did you find any hairpins?"

"Here."

Jacqueline jammed them into her chignon, seemingly at random, but the heavy coil remained miraculously in place. Jean rose to her feet, holding the purse.

"You missed the box of Band-Aids," Jacqueline said. "Behind the potted palm. And that's my rock, under the bust of Aristotle."

"Your rock," Jean repeated stupidly. She gathered up that item, and the Band-Aids, and an eyebrow pencil which had previously eluded her, and resisted the temptation to inquire whether Jacqueline didn't want Aristotle too. The cold green eyes fixed on her discouraged levity. But as she handed over the purse she couldn't resist saying,

"I used to think men were unfair when they made jokes about women's purses."

"I like to have things available." Jacqueline peered myopically into the purse. "I don't think you got everything, Jean. I don't see the flashlight, or that bottle of—"

"Maybe if you put your glasses on," Jean said, offering them.

"Don't I have them on? Oh. No, I don't. Thank you."

Jacqueline put the spectacles on, and Jean stared. The transformation was complete. Glasses, demure coiffure, modest dress—a well-bred middle-aged lady rooted through her overflowing handbag, muttering ladylike middle-aged epithets like "drat" and "blast."

"Hey," Michael said, grinning. "I think we've found a friend, Jean. Come on, Jacqueline. We'll buy you a drink, to settle your nerves."

"Why don't you have a slug of that?" Jean suggested, as Jacqueline, with a murmur of satisfaction, produced the miniature green bottle from the depths of the purse.

Jacqueline stared at her.

"Drink this? It's for my cat."

"Naturally," Michael said. "A feline aphrodisiac, no doubt. Or does it turn the cat into a woman, in the dark of the moon?"

"A little old lady in Trastevere makes it," Jacqueline said. "But it isn't really my cat. It—"

"It owns you. We know." Michael took her firmly by the elbow. "Come along, Jacqueline. You need something. I'm not sure what, but you'll have to settle for an espresso."

"Gino's?" Jean said uncertainly. "Michael, do you think the others will—"

"Don't let me intrude," Jacqueline said primly.

Tidy and bespectacled, she had the reserved dignity Jean associated with visiting maiden aunts and high-school Latin teachers. Jean found her formidable, quite a different person from the green-eyed witch sprawled across the Institute's marble floor. Michael was not intimidated. He took a firmer grip on Jacqueline's arm and said,

"The others will be fascinated."

As always, Jean was fascinated by the contrast between the grounds of the Institute and the street beyond the high enclosing wall. The Institute was housed in one of the stately old trans-Tiber villas, and its gardens were famous. The somber pointed cypresses and the famous umbrella pines formed a dark background for colorful masses of azaleas, bougainvillea, and oleander, and gave shade to the white marble benches scattered about.

The aristocratic villa withdrew, fastidiously, from the plebeian buildings which had sprung up around it, and from the crowded, noisy street. The shop fronts bore garish advertisements of the products to be found within, and the crumbling brown plaster of the walls carried copies of those proclamations to the citizenry in which the city government rejoiced. They were unsightly notices, flapping long tatters of dirty paper in the air, but Jean had never gotten over her thrill at the sight of the black initial letters which had two thousand years of dignity behind them. S.P.Q.R.—Senatus Populusque Romanus. The Senate and the People of Rome. Corrupt and crippled as the symbol had become, it still recalled the first great republic.

Gino's café was small and open-fronted, with a few rickety tables and chairs set out on the sidewalk. It had only one advantage over others in the area—the view. Located on top of a hill, it permitted its patrons to look out across a vista of trees and rooftops to where the dome of St. Peter's hovered among the clouds. In the opposite direction it was possible, on a clear day, to get a vision of the old city. Such days were rare; a gray fog of automobile exhaust shrouded the city of the Caesars most of the time.

As they plodded up the hill, Jean saw that three of her friends had already arrived at the café. Their faces were so familiar to her now that she never really looked at them. But today the presence of a stranger gave her a renewed and not wholly welcome insight. It was as if she had borrowed Jacqueline's glasses and acquired the owner's viewpoint with them.

One member of the group was conventional enough; Rome abounds in priests, of all sizes, nations, and degrees. Padre Ximenez wore the long black cassock which was *de rigueur* for his order while in the capital. Seeing him as a newcomer might, Jean was struck afresh by something she had unconsciously forced herself to ignore since the beginning of their friendship: José's dark Spanish features were strikingly handsome.

The Scovilles were brother and sister, although from a distance it was hard to tell which Scoville was which. The resemblance was superficial; a good deal of it resulted from the current fashions, or lack thereof. Anne wore the same faded jeans and tailored shirts as her brother. The red-gold Scoville hair resembled the coiffure affected by a number of well-known characters, among them Little Orphan Annie, Struwwelpeter, and Art Garfunkel. The coiffures were identical, except that Andy's hair was a little longer than his sister's. It framed Andy's face like a nimbus. There was nothing saintly about Andy's other features; it is difficult to imagine a saint with freckles, and Andy's blue eyes had the sparkle one associates with supernatural characters of the opposite persuasion. Beside him his sister looked drained and faded, as if she had contributed half the vitality which should have been hers to increase Andy's charm.

Michael had relapsed into one of his silent moods. He

dropped into the nearest chair and took out the sketch pad that went everywhere with him, leaving Jean to make the introductions and explain Jacqueline's presence. Andy found the story highly amusing. He broke into a loud guffaw, which ended abruptly as Jacqueline's basilisk stare fell upon him.

"I'm sorry," he muttered, with less than his usual aplomb. "It wasn't funny."

"Oh, it was," Jacqueline said gently. "If the custard-pie, pratfall school of comedy turns you on. . . . I'm not here by choice, you know. I was dragged. I'm not even sure I want to be here. What is this group of yours? A cell of an international conspiracy? A society for the prevention of something?"

The reactions of the three who were encountering Jacqueline's tongue for the first time were as varied as their personalities. Anne looked distressed. She was silent and shy at best, and controversy bothered her. José smiled. Andy, who had recognized a gift of restrained invective equal to his own, relaxed.

"If anything, we are a society for the encouragement of, not the prevention of, anything. We are part of the group, but not the whole. Our motto—"

"Shut up, Andy," Jean said equably. She looked at Jacqueline. "We just got into the habit of meeting here every morning for coffee. Four of us are student fellows. The Institute awards these fellowships, for a year's study in Rome—"

"I am well aware of that function of the Institute."

"Well, we four are this year's fellows. José is studying stained-glass design with one of the artists at the Institute, and the other two members of the crowd are also foreign students, who use the Institute library part of the time."

"Seven of you," Jacqueline said.

"It just happened that way. We really aren't a secret society."

"She thinks that's true," Andy said solemnly, "but she misses the point of numerology—the deeper meaning of it. We were Drawn Together. There is a Purpose in our coming here, from all over the world, to a meeting in the Center of it all."

"Hmmph," Jacqueline said. She edged her chair back in order to examine Andy more closely. Without looking up from his sketch, Michael grabbed her chair. Jacqueline gave him a startled glance and Jean said soothingly,

"Don't mind him. If he could talk he would tell you he's sketching you, and doesn't want you to move."

"Oh, he can talk; I've heard him. Why—"

"He's an artist," Andy said. There was a low growl from Michael, who continued to sketch, and Andy went on, "Painter, I should have said. They are real weirdos, these arty types. . . . All right, Michelangelo, but I have to call you something; would you prefer 'artistic?' No, I didn't think you would. . . . Anyhow, my own sister here happens to be one of them. She's a sculptor. And don't call her a sculptress, if you value your life. You wouldn't think people who work with their hands could get so hung up on words, would you?"

"Everybody is hung up on words," Jacqueline said. She smiled at Anne, who gave her a faint smile in return, but said nothing. "So Michael and Anne represent the 'art' half of the Institute for Art and Archaeology. You and Jean are the archaeologists, Andy?"

"The Institute discriminates against archaeologists," Andy said. "Jean is a compromise. An art historian."

"It averages out, over the years," Jean said earnestly. "They try to keep a balance."

"She is a compromise in several senses," José said, smiling at Jean. "She tries to keep the peace among us. It is not always easy."

"I believe you." Jacqueline's emerald eyes inspected him, an appraisal he met with smiling calm. The eyes moved on to examine Michael. Jacqueline's expression did not change, but Jean couldn't help wondering what she made of that young eccentric. He was about as aesthetic-looking as a wrestler. His features were heavy and blunt, with one exception, and only a keen observer would have noticed it—his mouth, thin-lipped and almost delicate in configuration. His hands were big, with thick, blunt-tipped fingers—the fingers of an artisan rather than an artist, according to the principles of palmistry. His heavy shoulders and habitual slouch made him look shorter than his actual height of nearly six feet. His shirt resembled the tie-dyed medleys so popular with young Americans, but Michael's rainbow version was not planned, it simply reflected the colors of his palettes over the past year. The shirt was open, not to the waist, but to a lower region where the band of Michael's faded jeans happened to have settled.

Jacqueline glanced over her shoulder at the entrance to the café. It gaped dark and forbidding as a cave mouth. There was no sign of life within.

"Where's our genial host?" she asked. "I could use

some coffee at that."

The concerted burst of laughter from the others made her eyebrows lift.

"Genial is such an appropriate word," said Andy, the self-appointed spokesman for the group. "Gino hates us all. I'd like to chalk it up to xenophobia, but I think he just doesn't like us personally."

"So he makes you wait," Jacqueline said musingly. She turned suddenly, and in a voice which could have been heard a block away, bellowed, *"Senta!"*

Everyone jumped except Michael, who was too far out in his own world to hear anything. Like a genie called by an incantation, Gino appeared in the doorway. His heavy black brows were drawn down in a formidable scowl; his unshaven jowls shone. The white apron draped across his paunch was stained with coffee, wine, and other unidentifiable marks. Jean suspected that he had been drawn out by outraged curiosity rather than zeal, but no one stopped to inquire into his motives.

"Un capuccino, per favore," Jacqueline said in a soft contralto. The others took advantage of Gino's speechless rage to give their orders, and after a comprehensive glower Gino vanished.

"Magnifico," José said admiringly. "Where did you learn to do that?"

"For ten years I was known as the loudest mom on the block," Jacqueline said complacently. "My children used to come home half an hour early to prevent me from letting out my famous voice."

"How many children do you have?" Jean asked.

"Two."

"Well? Aren't you going to show us their pictures?" Andy asked, glancing at the loaded purse squatting at Jacqueline's feet. A shapeless white lump, it looked alarmingly like the hideously animated leather bag that haunts one of M. R. James's most effective ghost stories; Jean kept expecting it to shoot out tiny withered arms and grab at someone's ankles.

"No. I'm not going to talk about them, either."

"Why not?"

"Because," said Jacqueline, glaring, "I have been talking about them and to them and with them and at them for twenty years. This is the first summer they've been on their own. I think they've survived my tutelage in fairly good shape, but I don't want to talk about them. Change the subject. Where are the other members of your secret society?"

Andy pointed dramatically.

"Peace, break thee off, look where they come," he misquoted.

Jean thought she would never again walk up that hill so unselfconsciously. The café provided a fine vantage point for a critical observer.

Small and slight and serious, Ted looked like a sixteen-year-old, with his heavy glasses and short, "square" haircut. But the long white scar on his forearm was the result of a bayonet cut acquired during the Six Days' War, and Ted was already respected in academic circles for his research on rock-cut tombs. He was a true sabra, a native-born Israeli; his father, a high-ranking government official and a hero of the 1948 war, lived in Tel Aviv. That was about all they knew of Ted's family history; he talked a blue streak about everything else, but not about himself.

Dana talked of very little else. In the first weeks after she joined the group the others heard so many references to hunting, and servants, and lawn tennis that they began to get suspicious. Finally Andy made a sarcastic comment about the upper classes, and Dana took the hint. When she forgot herself, her accent was strongly reminiscent of the Beatles' dulcet tones—straight Liverpudlian—and Jean imagined that betrayed Dana's real background.

Someone had told Jean once that she and Dana looked enough alike to be sisters. Her first reaction had been pleasure. A literal physical description could fit both girls—straight brown hair, dark eyes, round face, turned-up nose. They were approximately the same height, five feet five inches, but Dana weighed ten pounds more than Jean's one hundred and nine. This should have been a plus for Jean; she gained weight easily, and fought a constant battle with the pasta which is Italy's contribution to a limited student budget. But she had to admit Dana's extra poundage was distributed in the best possible way. The rest of Dana's features weren't particularly attractive; her complexion was rather muddy and her mouse-brown hair had none of the beauty of Ann's red-gold halo. Yet Dana exuded sex appeal, and Ann . . .

Social life requires a certain degree of hypocrisy. While these thoughts occupied her mind Jean greeted the newcomers and watched with a tight social smile as Dana wedged herself into a chair between Michael and Andy. Gino appeared with a tray and distributed cups. He was visibly sulking, and slammed most of the cups down with his usual heavy hand; but Jacqueline's *capuccino* was placed before her with delicate care.

José lifted his cup from the swimming saucer.

"Always my cup is the most mistreated," he announced gloomily. "Clearly Gino is anticlerical. Possibly a Communist."

"One need not be a Communist to be anticlerical," Ted said. "One must only be logical."

"My favorite adversary," the priest explained to Jacqueline. "You have perhaps noticed what a catholic group we are?"

"Catholic with a small *c*," Dana explained patronizingly.

"But of course. Catholic, with a capital *C,* Protestant, Jew, pagan—"

Andy bowed mockingly.

"And apostate," José concluded, with a nod at Michael, who went on sketching.

"You need a Moslem," Jacqueline said.

Andy let out a shout of laughter.

"I don't know who and what you are, lady, but you make a great straight man. You keep feeding me cues. Only I've already used the best line. All I can say is— brace yourselves. Here he comes."

Jean turned her head. Midway up the hill she saw the figure to which Andy pointed.

"It's only Albert," she said resignedly. "What a ham you are, Andy."

"Who is Albert?" Jacqueline asked. "Another of the group?"

"No, I told you it was a mystic number. The Seven Sinners."

"Why sinners?"

"The name is Andy's invention," Ted explained. "He thinks it is funny. He has a primitive sense of humor."

"But we're all sinners," Andy declared. "All miserable sinners, in a sinful world. Right, José?"

The priest raised his eyes heavenward and sighed loudly. Andy went on,

"Albert is one of our crosses. We bear him patiently because we are trying to improve ourselves. Albert was sent to us so we could practice on him. If we ever learn to love Albert, we can love anything."

Jacqueline adjusted her glasses, which had a tendency to slip, and stared at the plodding figure.

"What's wrong with him? Or are you just anti-Moslem?"

"He is not a Moslem," Ted said coolly. "As usual, Andy is inaccurate. He is a Maronite—a Lebanese Christian. And we have Andy to thank for his charming presence among us—another sin on Andy's extensive list. They were boyhood friends in Beirut."

"Friends, hell," Andy protested. "His old man and my old man taught at the American University years ago, and we went to the same school. Don't hassle me, Ted; Albert would have forced himself on us even if he'd never seen any of us before. That's the kind of creep he is."

No one replied. The newcomer was now upon them.

Jean had to admit that Albert was not only ugly, he was unprepossessing. The two qualities are not necessarily synonymous. Physical ugliness can be appealing, even attractive. She had seen homelier men than Albert—though not many. He had not a single redeeming feature.

His scanty forehead was half hidden by greasy locks of black hair. His face was deeply pitted with the scars of acne. In order to accommodate his protruding front teeth his upper lip had stretched to an unbelievable degree; in profile his face looked anthropoid, chinless and loose-lipped. He was also fat—not chubby or plump, but flabbily obese. Like Michael he wore his belt around his hips instead of his waist, but while gravity pulled Michael's belt down his lean body, Albert's immense paunch eliminated his waistline altogether. He had small, squinting eyes, which were buried, when he smiled, between his fat cheeks and his overhanging brows. The worn leather briefcase he carried wherever he went seemed to drag one shoulder down, so that he walked with an odd lurch.

Yet it was not Albert's looks that made him repulsive; it was his manner. He exuded spiritual malaise like a bad smell. Consciously Jean felt sorry for him, but when he dragged a chair next to hers and patted her on the knee with a pudgy paw, she had to force herself to smile back at him instead of pulling away as from a leper.

One of Albert's maddening, yet pathetic, qualities was his unawareness of how he affected people. His face shone greasily as he greeted them. Tenderly he stowed his briefcase under his chair. The squinting eyes inspected them, lingering longest on Jean and on Dana—who responded with a curl of her lip—and then discovered Jacqueline.

"Albert Gébara," he announced, giving the first name the French pronunciation.

"How do you do. I'm Jacqueline Kirby."

"Not a student," said Albert, eyeing her. "Too old, eh?

Madame ou mademoiselle Kirby? Docteur, peut-être?"

"Just Jacqueline."

"Mais non, ce n'est pas bien de parler à une dame d'un certain âge—"

Andy groaned.

"Our tactful Albert. Look, you *crétin,* don't you know it isn't polite to refer to a lady's age? And for God's sake speak English. You can if you want to. Sort of . . . It's rude to use a language the people you're with don't understand."

Albert's beady eyes remained fixed on Jacqueline.

"Mais vous comprenez français, vous comprenez fort bien ce que je vous dis—"

"Un peu," Jacqueline admitted cautiously.

"Alors. Madame Kirby? Madame la professeur? Madame la—"

"No," Jacqueline said. "I'm not a teacher. I'm a librarian."

"Une bibliothécaire." Albert nodded with satisfaction. He got up, taking his chair and his briefcase with him, and moved around the table to sit next to Jacqueline. Under cover of the ensuing conversation Andy muttered,

"Thank God, somebody else who speaks French. I was getting tired of being the sole recipient of Albert's confidences. His conversational style has its points, though; he gets the information. A librarian! I wouldn't have figured it."

"You wouldn't?" Dana didn't bother to lower her voice. "Men are so unobservant. I spotted her at once. Dull, dreary, and middle-class."

"Unlike you," said Andy. "A model of courtesy; that's

our Dana."

Dana subsided. Andy was the only one who could squelch her effectively.

Albert was now in full spate. He was speaking English; apparently Jacqueline's "little" French had failed her. Conversation died in Albert's presence; his loud tones overwhelmed other voices, and his remarks were so outrageous that they held his auditors in a spell of unwilling fascination.

"I am Christian, you understand," he explained to an incredulous Jacqueline. "You think me dirty Moslem, perhaps. But I am—"

"No," Jacqueline said. "Not exactly."

The sarcasm was lost on Albert.

"Not a dirty Moslem," he repeated, lingering pleasurably on the word. "Good Christian, true Christian. I love Holy Mother of God, all the saints. I come here, I work, I study, for the blessed saints. The Church not good Christian. No good now. Need good Christian like me to make better."

Jacqueline glanced at José, but got no support from that source; the priest's eyes looked glazed.

"You are going to improve the Church?" Jacqueline repeated. "In what way?"

Albert patted her approvingly on the knee. He clearly had a fetish about that part of the female anatomy.

"Save saints," Albert explained. "The Church say not— she say—*à renoncer les saints. Mais les histoires des saints sont incontestables. Les saints—*"

"It is the bee in his bonnet," said José, no longer able to restrain himself. He spoke directly to Jacqueline, as if he

26

were trying to deny Albert's existence. "He refers to the revision of the calendar of saints several years ago; and I cannot seem to make him understand that there is no rejection of those saints who were removed. They may still be venerated, still receive devotions. But the legends—"

"No, no, you are wrong," said Albert, with his usual tact—and with a command of English which increased miraculously whenever he wished to voice a direct insult or contradiction. "You are stupid. The Church deny—that is right word, deny—older saints. Saint Christopher, Saint Barbara, *les autres.* All true. All real. I prove. The Pope is wrong, stupid, like you."

"I hate to agree, but I never did forgive the Holy Father for dumping Christopher." Michael looked up from his drawing. He had a disconcerting habit of reentering a conversation after a long silence, with a remark that proved he had been paying attention after all. "The week after he was kicked out, I ran my cycle into a tree."

The comment struck the right note. José grinned unwillingly and relaxed.

"I grant that you on a motorcycle need all the help you can get, Michael. But the legends of such saints were long overdue for reappraisal. It is not heretical to question such stories, the Church itself does so. Early theologians were untrained in historical method; they misinterpreted—"

"No, no, no," said Albert. "No misinterpret. All true. Truth comes from God, only God. We know truth already. But heretics need proof. I find."

"Albert," said Andy, "why don't you shut up?"

Albert beamed at him.

"I find proof. Seven virgin saints—"

José put both hands on the table, as if he were trying to keep them in sight so they wouldn't get away from him and commit violence.

"There are not seven virgin saints," he said, between his beautiful white teeth. "There are hundreds of virgin saints. Or forty-two, or nine, or none at all. But not seven. It is a magic number, a relic of paganism—"

"Seven," said Albert obdurately. "I prove."

He dragged the bulging briefcase out from under his chair and began fumbling with the catch.

Andy stood up.

"I'm copping out," he announced. "I have had it. So long, troops."

"Me too," Dana said. "I'm not in the mood to discuss virginity today. Going back to the library, José?"

One by one they got to their feet, collecting their belongings, settling their destinations. Albert continued to talk. Jean knew he would trail them, talking, all the way back to the Institute. Clutching his briefcase to his ample chest, he started to rise.

Jacqueline turned.

"You cannot come," she announced, in the same voice that had electrified Gino. "I don't want to talk to you any more today. Stay here. We will talk another day. Goodbye."

She put her hand on Albert's shoulder and shoved him down into his chair. He was sitting there, his mouth ajar, as the others fled.

Jean found herself walking with Jacqueline. After a moment she realized that someone was singing softly. It took several more moments to decide that the sound was in fact coming from the bland, dignified person at her side; it was that ditty beloved of the young radical, "The Times They Are a-Changing."

"'The battle outside rages,'" crooned Jacqueline. Catching Jean's look, she broke off and inquired suavely, "Am I embarrassing you?"

"Why should I be embarrassed?"

"My daughter always was. Between the ages of twelve and seventeen she never walked beside me in public."

"You didn't sing all the time, did you?" asked Jean, willing, by now, to believe it.

"No, but she never knew when I was going to burst out. It was worst at Christmas. I love Christmas carols."

"And Bob Dylan?"

"And Salvation Army hymns, German lieder, and song hits of the nineteen forties. I know all the words. I know," said Jacqueline proudly, "more totally useless things than anyone you'll ever meet."

"Not everything you know is useless. You disposed of Albert beautifully." Jean glanced at her companion's rather bony profile, saw an encouraging gleam of humor in the one visible green eye, and said, without premeditation, "I can't figure you out. How many people are you?"

"You can't be that young," said Jacqueline contemptuously. "Don't you know that every human being is at least a dozen different people? I'm indulging myself this summer, and letting them all hang out, as Michael would say. When I'm working I'm not so visibly schizophrenic."

Having reached the gates of the Institute, the group stopped to reorganize itself. Turning, Jean realized that

José, walking behind them, had been listening to the conversation. His dark eyes were intent on Jacqueline.

"You have just voiced a great truth," he said.

"About schizophrenia?" Jacqueline didn't smile.

"About the complexity of personality. Half the trouble in human relations arises from expecting human beings to conform to a single one-dimensional image. We are all hydra-headed monsters. But most people never learn that."

With an abrupt nod he strode off, his long black skirts flapping. Ted ran to join him, tossing a casual word of farewell over his shoulder. The others lingered.

"Stick around, Jake," Andy invited. "We may need you, if Albert materializes again."

"I," said Jacqueline, ignoring the nickname, "am lunching with your hereditary enemy, the distinguished librarian of the Institute. She hates to be kept waiting, and I am already late."

"She's a friend of yours?" Andy demanded incredulously.

Jacqueline's lips quivered.

"She sees only one of my numerous images. It matches hers—dignified, prim, and passionately interested in the deficiencies of the Dewey Decimal System."

"Andy is supposed to be passionately interested in the archaeology of Rome," Ann said firmly. "Come on, boy. Dad is arriving next week, and your report to the fellowship committee had better be finished by then."

"Damnably true," Andy admitted, with a groan. "And if the résumé isn't turned in I won't get my fellowship renewed, and then dear old Dad will murder me."

"Your father is coming?" Dana's eyes widened "Wow! I've got to meet him, Andy. He's the most glamorous figure in our field."

"And glamorous archaeologists are rare," Jean said drily. "He's a brilliant scholar—"

"Brilliant, hell. He's got dash—panache. That photo of him dangling over the cliff in Iran, at the end of a rope—"

"Panache is right," Andy muttered. "The Behistun inscription has been copied a hundred times. Sam only did it to show off."

"And the workman he rescued from the rockfall at Tiryns?" Jean demanded. "That was showing off?"

"And the book on pre-Attic pottery," Dana said.

"All right, so you're all members of the fan club. I'll arrange a soirée. . . . Hey, that's a good idea. We'll have a party and some of you fans can pitch in and keep him entertained. He needs an audience the way some people need insulin. He goes into a coma without it."

"Don't mind him," Ann said, with a nervous smile. "He thinks Sam is great, really. Come *on,* brother. Work. W-O-R-K. Remember?"

They went off, arm in arm, and Michael, watching them, said lazily, "There's something allegorical about those two."

"Beauty and the Beast," suggested Dana, with a giggle. "Or how about Orestes and Electra? There's a nice normal brother-sister team for you."

Michael gave her a smack on the bottom that echoed like a pistol shot. She yelped. Jean, hoping to prevent further horseplay under Jacqueline's cynical eye, said at random, "How about the Bobbsey twins? I never can remember their names—"

"Nan and Bert," said Jacqueline. "That's enough of that. What a nasty-tongued bunch you are. . . . Michael, let me see that sketch you made of me."

"Huh?" Michael retreated, clutching his sketch pad. "Be damned if I will."

"Undoubtedly. Hand it over."

With a shrug, Michael obeyed. Jacqueline studied the page in grim silence. Jean couldn't resist. Craning, she looked over Jacqueline's shoulder.

Michael hadn't done one sketch; the page was covered with small figures. Jacqueline sprawled on the floor of the Institute, like a marble figure on a somewhat risqué tomb; Jacqueline telling someone off, mouth wide open, finger raised; Jacqueline peering over the top of her glasses, looking quite feeble-minded; Jacqueline wearing the helmet and breastplate of Minerva, and her own horn-rimmed glasses; Jacqueline wearing nothing at all, in the classic pose of the Venus of Cyrene.

Dana was making strangled sounds of stifled amusement, but Jean didn't find the sketch funny, even though the individual portraits were wonderful caricatures. Michael could have overheard Jacqueline's remarks about multiple personality; but the sketch had been finished before the conversation took place. At times Michael's insights verged frighteningly on clairvoyance. He had sketched all his friends at one time or another. Dana was a favorite victim, which explained her delight in another victim's unveiling.

Finally Jacqueline returned the sketch. She gave Michael a long, steady look. There was no amusement in

32

her face, nor was there resentment. When she spoke, Jean knew she wasn't joking.

"You're lucky to be living in this century, Michael. Five hundred years ago they'd have burned you at the stake. And I'd have been in the audience, poking the fire."

TWO

THE next day Jean was seized by one of those productive fits which strike only too rarely. She worked in a grim fog, resisting the blandishments of her friends. Since the library of the Institute was one of the few places in Rome that kept American hours, she could work straight through from early morning till eight at night. It was at that hour, a week later, that the attack passed, leaving her blinking blearily at a page covered with words which suddenly looked as meaningless as hieroglyphs. Her stomach was a cavernous complaint, and her head felt as if it were floating several inches away from her neck.

Jean gathered her papers together in an untidy pile and left her office. She was starving, and not only for food; she wanted company, laughter and conversation, a glass of wine, an enormous plate of spaghetti alla bolognese, twelve hours' sleep, and a bath—not necessarily in that order. None of these reasonable desires seemed to be immediately available. The nearest trattoria was half a mile away, and all her erstwhile friends seemed to have vanished.

As she approached the stairs, one of the office doors

opened. Jean stopped. The hall was dimly lit, but she recognized the smooth helmet of bronze hair and the bulky lump of the purse. It seemed to have gained in weight and girth since she had seen it last, and she wondered what incongruous objects it now contained.

"Good evening," Jacqueline Kirby said. "You look like an underdone biscuit. How are you?"

"Fine." The word came out as an unconvincing croak, and Jean cleared her throat. "I'm just hungry. I've been working for . . . What day is it?"

"Friday. I know you've been working; I've been watching you." There was more envy than commiseration in Jacqueline's voice. "I could do it too, when I was your age. That and a lot of other things that are no longer within my capabilities. . . . Want a ride home? Or are you going directly to Andy's?"

"I feel fine," Jean repeated vaguely. She was thinking about the last paragraph she had written. Then, belatedly, a fact penetrated the lingering fog of scholarship.

"Andy's? Andy's party! For his father . . . Has he gone?"

"Who? Where?"

"Andy. He was in his office all afternoon."

"He left at five, to get ready for the party."

"Yes, the party." Jean shook herself. "Lord, I am shot! I've got to hurry. Gosh. I look like . . . What time is it?"

"Calm down. The party doesn't start till nine, which means it won't get interesting until about ten. You have plenty of time to repair the ravages of hard labor."

"What about you?" Jean shook her head. "I seem to be saying the most stupid things tonight. I mean, you look fine the way you are. You don't need—"

"At my age there isn't much I can do anyway," Jacqueline said sadly. "Still, I suppose I should make an effort. . . . Do you want a ride or don't you?"

Jean looked at her, saw the twinkle in her eye, and relaxed.

"Thank you. I would, if it isn't out of your way. I didn't know you had a car."

"You've missed a lot the last few days. While you were in your fog, my friend Frau Hilman went off on vacation, leaving me her car and her apartment."

"It's nice to have friends."

"She also left me her Persian cat, her pink poodle, and a tank of assorted and delicate tropical fish. By the time I dredge the cat out of the fish tank and chop the poodle's daily gourmet dinner, I begin to wonder whether I made such a good deal."

They emerged from the building into the balmy dusk of a Roman night, and Jean took a deep, restorative breath.

"The car's down this way," Jacqueline said. She hesitated, and then said, almost reluctantly, "Would you like to come back with me and have scrambled eggs or something? There's also a shower. I'm not trying to sound like a TV commercial for soap, but I've lived in student lodgings myself, and I know about those little washbasins in the corner of the room, the kind with two cold water taps."

"That's very nice of you," Jean said.

"Oh, nice is the word for me," Jacqueline agreed sarcastically. She turned the key in the ignition and was rewarded by a peculiar grinding noise. Looking flustered, she made movements with her feet; the noise subsided into a dull roar. "I hate this car," she muttered. "I hate driving in Rome."

"Why do you do it?"

"Masochism. In New England we call it self-discipline, but it's the same thing." The car jerked out into traffic, and Jacqueline relaxed a trifle. "Luckily, the Institute and the apartment are both on this side of the river. If I had to fight my way through that maze of streets in the old city, I'd chicken out."

"Are you sure you want me to come?" Jean asked.

"Why not?"

It was not a particularly gracious reply, but the tone reassured Jean.

"Could we stop by my place and let me get a clean outfit? I live just off the Via di San Pancrazio."

"Sure."

It took Jean approximately three minutes to go up to her room and come back. Her chauffeur regarded her with respect.

"That was fast."

"I've only got one clean dress."

They retraced their route, getting lost only once. At this point Jacqueline commented pungently, and it was Jean's turn to look at her with respect.

"You don't sound like a librarian," she said.

"I'm on vacation." Jacqueline laughed. "Well, I suppose there is an image, isn't there? But stereotypes are awfully misleading. There are typical librarians, but not all librarians are typical. Any more than any other profession."

"Such as archaeology," Jean agreed. "From what I've heard about him, Dr. Scoville isn't typical."

"Oh, yeah? The swinging anthropologist is a subcategory of the general stereotype. The ivory-tower image irks some scholars; they have to prove they are just as much with it as the next man, just as brilliant about contemporary issues as they are in their specialty."

"I don't think Dr. Scoville is trying to prove anything."

"Oh, dear, I'm attacking one of your heroes," Jacqueline said sweetly. "On the surface he appears to have everything—sex appeal, virility, scholarly prestige, popular charm. But maybe the really basic thing about the man is that he gets bilious when he eats onions, and has to pull in his stomach when he looks at himself in the mirror. This would explain his deeds of derring-do, which, you must admit, verge occasionally on exhibitionism."

Jean studied her companion's calm profile in amazement.

"I don't think I've ever heard anything more cynical in my life."

"You're young yet."

Jacqueline turned the car into a dark, narrow street, lined on both sides with high walls. She switched on the headlights; in the modern, well-lit streets she had used only the driving lights prescribed by Roman law. Jean said, "I don't think I've been this way."

"This is the old Via Aurelia," Jacqueline said. They both winced as a car roared toward them and passed without, to their mutual surprise, any scraping of fenders. "It's hard for me to drive it; I always want to climb the right-hand wall when I meet another car. But the very name thrills me."

"I'm glad to see you're not a hardened cynic."

"I'm only cynical about people. Places and things still

make me go all soft like a jelly doughnut. That's a sign of middle age, if you like."

The walls disappeared, to be replaced by new apartment buildings; the street widened, and the romance died. Jacqueline made several more turns, following a maze of side streets, and finally drove through a narrow entranceway which was marked "private." There was a small lodge; a *portiere* came out, recognized the car, and returned to his dinner.

"Wow," Jean said. "I didn't know library work paid this well."

The drive led into one of the private apartment complexes which were becoming common in the new subdivisions of the city. The only car entrance was the one through which they had come, with its guard on duty to question tradesmen and uninvited guests. Unlike the big blocklike apartments for lower-cost living, this complex had only four apartments to a building, and these were scattered at random through a handsomely landscaped park. Even the poorest Roman apartment has one balcony; these had five or six. As they followed the private drive, past bushes of evergreens and azaleas, Jean saw that the soft shaded lights in the center of the compound illumined a large swimming pool, its waters glowing soft blue-green.

"Wow," she said again.

"Wow indeed." Jacqueline slid the car into a slot between a low-slung European sports car and a Cadillac limousine. "Don't get any wild ideas. Lise has a private income in addition to her salary. Come along; you ain't seen nothing yet."

The building had an elevator, which did not open until Jacqueline inserted a key into the door lock. Above, it opened directly into the foyer of the apartment. This room, which was larger than Jean's bedroom, was marble-floored. The marble extended into the *salone,* or living-dining area, which occupied the entire front of the building. One curving wall was all windows, with two French doors opening onto the long front balcony. Through the glass Jean could see masses of flowers, geraniums and plumbago and roses, in boxes along the balcony rail. Beyond, the shimmering acquamarine shape of the pool looked like a magnified jewel.

Feeling particularly grubby, Jean followed her hostess into the room, which was furnished with oriental rugs and heavily carved and gilded rococo furniture. The ambulatory part of the menagerie was waiting for them. The cat, a big ball of silver fur, blinked green eyes at them and remained on the brocade-covered couch. The poodle was really pink. It bounced across the floor, yelping shrilly, and made a dive at Jean's ankles.

"*Nein,* Prinz," Jacqueline said firmly.

The dog rolled over, with its miniature paws dangling. A ribbon, of a rosy shade slightly darker than its curls, was tied around its topknot.

"Poor little thing," Jean said, bending over to scratch the exposed stomach. "Why do poodles always strike me as pathetic?"

"He's really a nice little guy," Jacqueline said; the poodle responded by wriggling and licking Jean's bare toes. "People tend to treat them like toys instead of dogs, that's why they're pathetic. Nothing pathetic about Nefertiti over there; she rules the roost, and she knows it."

The cat blinked again. Its expression was one of concentrated contempt.

When Jean had finished her shower she found Jacqueline in the kitchen. The poodle was lying at her feet making suggestive whining noises. Nefertiti sat on the table. The cat's eyes were on a level with Jacqueline's as she sat beside the table, and the expressions on the two faces, feline and human, were so much alike that Jean couldn't repress a burst of laughter.

"Quiet," Jacqueline said, without turning her head. "I'm trying to outstare her."

Then Jean saw the bottle. It was the same small green bottle she had seen once before. There was a medicine dropper beside it.

"It really is for the cat," she exclaimed.

"I said it was, didn't I? It's a tonic. Lise swears by it. Personally I think this animal needs tranquilizers instead of vitamins, but . . . Look, would you mind holding her back legs?"

The struggle would have been funny if it hadn't been so painful. Jean had two bleeding scratches on her forearms before it was over, and Jacqueline was liberally spattered with green liquid. It smelled like mint and was very sticky. The cat retired, spitting and drooling greenly, and Jacqueline directed a few well-chosen words at its furry rear. She fed the dog and sprinkled a handful of food in the fish tank in the *salone*. Then, with a martyred sigh, she began to scramble eggs.

They ate scrambled eggs with chopped prosciutto, salad, and fresh rolls with a soft cream cheese that came in little cardboard pots. The shower had increased Jean's appetite. Only when her plate was scraped clean did she take a deep breath and apologize for gluttony.

"Want coffee?" Jacqueline asked.

Jean looked at her watch.

"Hadn't we better go?"

"There's no hurry." Jacqueline got up and filled two coffee cups, which she brought to the table. "You really haven't been with it the last few days, have you?"

"Why? Has something happened?"

"Yes and no. Maybe it's just my imagination getting out of hand." Jacqueline sighed. "I've always been very square about things such as grades, and doing well in school. But lately I'm beginning to wonder whether your contemporaries who complain about academic pressure haven't got a point. Does the renewal of your fellowships really mean that much to you? I mean 'you' plural."

"I wouldn't say so," Jean said slowly. "In fact, I think I'm the only one who's uptight about it. Michael really doesn't care; he's so far out, nothing bothers him. He'd live in a cave if it had a northern light. Have you seen his room?"

"No."

"Well, it's the most incredible mess. . . . He picked it because it has a skylight. Ice forms on things in the winter, and in summer it's like walking into a Turkish bath. He has to keep the skylight open to get some air; the roof is a playground for little kids, and a place where the teen-agers go to make out, and a breeding ground for a tribe of wild Roman cats. If the kids aren't howling obscenities through the skylight, the cats are making messes through it, or some ardent Casanova is falling through it. Literally. One dazed kid crashed right through one night, and landed on top of Michael's latest painting, which wasn't dry. . . . All right, it sounds funny, I know, but the funniest thing is that Michael doesn't even *notice*. Oh, he noticed the boy who fell on his painting, but only because he smeared it. How he could tell the difference I don't know."

"He's a nonrepresentational painter?" Jacqueline asked, through her laughter.

"You might call it that. I haven't seen much of his work; he's very secretive about letting people see it. He says he hates criticism. He does, too. He's supposed to be studying with Professor Lugetti, but he won't let the man in to look at his paintings. Michael has a studio at the Institute. Every few weeks Lugetti gets mad and forces his way into the studio, and you can hear the argument all over the building. They stand there and scream at each other for about an hour and then Lugetti stamps out, cursing in Italian, and Michael jumps up and down cursing in English."

"Lugetti's temper is a byword," Jacqueline said. "I'm surprised he doesn't throw Michael out of the place."

"That's what's so funny. He swears Michael is the hottest talent since Monet."

"I admit Michael doesn't sound like the worrying type. What about the others?"

"José and Ted and Dana aren't Fellows. I suppose they have their private worries—who doesn't?—but the renewal problem isn't bugging them."

"Aren't they here on some kind of scholarship aid?"

"Dana is pretty vague about her means of support; I think her family is staking her."

"José is being sponsored by his college?"

"College?"

"He's a Jesuit, isn't he?"

"Right. He doesn't need to worry about money then, does he?"

"No, I suppose not. Not money . . . And Ted?"

"It's funny," Jean said, frowning, "but we never talk about things like that. . . . I guess he's got a grant from the government or something. I do get the feeling he's been having personal worries. He hardly ever talks about himself, but he's engaged, to a girl back home. When he first came, he talked about her quite a bit. Showed us her picture, and all that. Lately he hasn't mentioned her. Let's see, who else is there? Oh, the Gold Dust twins."

"Do you call them that? I didn't think any of you remembered that old advertising gimmick."

"Ann mentioned the phrase. I think she's self-conscious about their closeness. They look enough alike to be twins, but she's a year older than Andy."

"Isn't it unusual to have a brother and sister both Fellows of the Institute, in the same year?"

"Well . . ." Jean scraped crumbs into a neat pile with her forefinger. "I think they're both talented. But—it's a practical world, isn't it? And Dr. Scoville has a lot of friends in the archaeology business."

"I'm glad to see you aren't as naïve as you look. How good are the Scovilles, really? Be honest—if you can."

"I can't judge Ann's work, it's not my field," Jean said defensively. "But I happen to know Andy's doctoral dissertation was a really brilliant piece of work. The university wanted to publish it, and they don't do that with many dissertations."

"Andy has his doctorate?"

"Yes, he got it at some incredible age—twenty-one or twenty-two. But he doesn't like to be called Doctor. He's very modest."

"No academic worries for Andy, then."

"Oh, no. If anyone gets his fellowship renewed, it will be Andy. Look, Jacqueline, I don't want to rush you, but—"

"Don't be polite," Jacqueline said, in the deceptively gentle voice Jean was beginning to know, and dread. "Just tell me outright you think I'm a nosy old gossip."

"No," Jean admitted. "You aren't a gossip. Something's bugging you. What is it?"

"I definitely do not believe in premonitions," Jacqueline said, half to herself. "But there's an atmosphere. . . . You get so you can feel it in your bones. Like earthquake weather."

"Premonitions, intuition—I believe in them, but they're always based on some real fact your conscious mind hasn't recognized. Something must have happened to set you off."

The kitchen light gleamed off Jacqueline's bronze hair and drained her face of much of its color.

"Your friend Albert, for one thing. It seems he's disappeared."

Ann and Andy had an apartment in Trastevere. Their father, who had had considerable success as a writer of popular nonfiction, was contributing to their income; the stipend awarded to Fellows barely covered the cost of a room in a cheap boardinghouse. Formerly a working-class district of questionable repute, Trastevere was now considered picturesque. A trip to its night spots was on the agenda of many tourists. Luckily the wide-eyed tourists, in their drip-dry nylon dresses and lightweight business suits, couldn't understand the comments hurled at them by barefoot students and harassed waiters.

With his linguistic gifts and ready sympathy, Andy had made himself part of the local scene almost from the first. Andy's friends reaped the rewards of his popularity. Parking is a problem anywhere in Rome. In Trastevere it is a joke. When Jean and Jacqueline arrived, they found the street completely filled; there were cars parked in every available space, including those marked by the slashed red circle signs which indicate that parking is forbidden, and even the sidewalks were littered with Vespas, motorbikes, and ordinary bicycles. Jacqueline was looking around in dismay when a young man sauntered up and put his head in the window.

"Friends of Andy's? Leave the car, signora, I will take care of it."

"It's all right," Jean said. "This is Alberto Sordi; he's an engineering student. Alberto, this is Signora Kirby."

Alberto managed to bow without taking his head out of the window—a feat which only an Italian can accomplish. Jacqueline gave her companion a dubious look, but she got out, leaving the keys in the car.

"It isn't my car," she said apprehensively. "You will be careful . . . ?"

Alberto, hand on his heart, made a more sweeping bow.

"Signora, if there is a scratch, anywhere, tomorrow, you may inflict a corresponding wound on my body."

Jacqueline looked startled at this effusion, and Jean, who knew they were being royally kidded, took the older woman's arm.

"Andy probably will do just that," she told Alberto, and grinned unwillingly as a look of exaggerated terror replaced that worthy's broad smile. "Thanks, Alberto. See you later."

She pulled Jacqueline into the doorway of the building as Alberto leaped eagerly into the driver's seat. Jean knew he would live up to his promise; the car wouldn't have a mark on it when he returned it. But it would be well for Jacqueline's nerves if she didn't see how he drove.

The Scovilles had the top floor, the most desirable part of the building because of the wide terrace that surrounded it on three sides. But the top floor was the sixth, and there was no elevator. As they climbed, the sounds of the party became louder and clearer.

"I wonder the neighbors don't complain," Jacqueline said, panting.

"Nobody in Trastevere complains about parties. They all come out on the landing and enjoy the noise. . . . *Buona sera, signora . . . signori. . . .*"

The last remark was addressed to the inhabitants of one of the fifth-floor apartments, who were standing in their open doorway, nodding and tapping their feet in time to the music.

They were the last of the crowd to arrive. Ximenez caught Jean's eye first; his severe black was conspicuous among the gay costumes of the others, both male and female. There was another priest present; his cassock was the bright scarlet worn by German clerics while in Rome.

In honor of the occasion Ann was wearing a dress—or perhaps it was one of her brother's shirts. Severely tailored, a solid green in color, it reached only to the tops of her thighs and displayed legs which, as Jean had noticed before, were attractively shaped. Ann made no further concessions to femininity; she stood with her usual slouch as she faced Ted, with whom she was carrying on an animated conversation.

Jean's eyes swept the room. There was Michael, sitting on the floor in the corner. His knees were drawn up and his bare feet had charcoal-gray soles. He held a glass of wine in both hands, and he looked sulky, withdrawn, rather like an autistic patient squatting in a hospital corridor.

For once Dana wasn't with him, and Jean located the other girl where she had expected her to be—hovering at the elbow of a tall, gray-haired man whom Jean recognized from his pictures and from his resemblance to his son.

Dana was dressed to catch the eye. Wide gold hoops glittered against the masses of her dark hair, and an off-the-shoulder white blouse carried out the gypsy look which was now fashionable. Blazing scarlet, electric blue, wide stripes of chartreuse and orange contributed to her layers of skirts; a sash of purple encircled her waist, and she jangled with bracelets and necklaces.

She was not the only acolyte worshiping at the famous scholar's shrine. He was surrounded by people, Andy's student friends and two of the older Fellows from the Institute. He towered above them physically. His gray hair was cut short. Burned brown by the eastern suns of successive winter digs, he looked twenty years younger than his real age, and his broad shoulders were those of a man who has done his share of the punishing physical work required on an archaeological excavation.

The contrast between his casual but conventional white shirt and dark slacks and Andy's peacock-colored clothing was as extreme as the difference in their complexions, but the resemblance was there—not only in the features of the long, clean-cut faces but in the crackling vitality that animated those faces. Andy was on the fringe of the group near his father, but he was not part of it. Lounging against the wall, he held a half-filled glass, and the expression on his face as he watched his father was one of patronizing amusement. He turned his head, saw the newcomers, and bounded toward them, emitting cries of welcome.

"I gave you up," he said to Jean.

The blue eyes met hers with an intensity that cut the two of them off from the rest of the room. Then Andy remembered his manners. He turned to Jacqueline. "You look beautiful. Come on and meet the great man."

Jacqueline gave Jean a look of half-comic appeal as she was drawn away, but Jean refused to respond; the great man had too many panting females in his entourage as it was.

She wandered over to the refreshment table and helped herself to a glass of wine. She was joined at once by Ximenez, who greeted her with pleasure.

"You have been working too hard," he said. "We missed you at our daily meetings; you are our peacemaker, you know."

"From what Jacqueline tells me, you haven't needed much arbitration," Jean said; and then, at José's look of bewilderment, she elaborated. "Albert. Jacqueline says he's disappeared."

"Disappeared? What a word." Ann's cool voice broke in.

"He was strange that last day we saw him," José said thoughtfully. "Outside of himself."

The odd phrase struck Jean disagreeably.

"What do you mean?"

José's black eyes narrowed thoughtfully.

"It is hard to describe. Excited? That is not quite the word. There is an English word—'fey.' Perhaps I do not understand its correct meaning. . . ."

"I hope not. It has something to do with a premonition of approaching doom."

"It also means crazy," Ann said irritably. "For God's sake, you all talk as if he'd vanished in a cloud of smoke, in front of sixty witnesses. Why make such a big thing of it?"

"Right on. Let's not talk about awful Albert." Michael had joined the group. "Hey, José, have you seen the watercolors at that new gallery on the Via Margutta?"

José had. The conversation became too technical for Jean, who was not in the mood for shoptalk after her days of strenuous study. Turning, she caught Andy's eye. She had the feeling he had been watching her for some time, and she felt herself flushing absurdly, like a schoolgirl.

Andy was the only male in the group who could affect her so. Ted and José were good friends. Michael? There was a potential spark in that relationship, but Michael was too emotionally unstable for Jean. He was definitely the flitting type—from flower to flower to flower. Andy was something else. When he summoned her, with a smile and a slight movement of his head, Jean obeyed.

"Having fun?" he asked softly. The words were trivial, but the tone, and the look that accompanied it, invested the commonplace phrase with special meaning.

"It's a good party, Andy. Everyone is having fun."

"Including our Jacqueline," Andy said, grinning. "Dig that technique, will you?"

Jean turned her head and saw Jacqueline and Scoville Senior walking toward the doors that opened onto the terrace. Jacqueline's dignified librarian friend would have had difficulty recognizing her in her present costume; the jade-green of her fashionable pants suit darkened her eyes to emerald, and set off her slim figure. Her hair was coiled around her head like a metallic wreath. As she smiled at her tall companion, whose head was bent attentively, Jean saw with amusement that Jacqueline's glasses were no longer in evidence. Only one item detracted from an otherwise perfect vision of sophisticated elegance: the Purse. Jean found that she was thinking of it in capital letters.

The couple vanished into the darkness of the terrace, and Andy laughed aloud.

"She lifted him right out from under Dana's nose," he said admiringly. "Our Dana is losing her touch."

Jean started to answer; but the words caught in her throat as she saw the change in Andy's face. He was staring past her at the doorway. Jean whirled around, expecting some cataclysmic vision. Her eyes fell upon an object which, if unsightly, did not at first glance seem horrifying enough to explain Andy's consternation. It was only Albert, returned from his temporary absence.

Albert's presence never produced ecstasies of joyful welcome; but now the silence that gradually spread through the room, freezing the guests in mid-sentence and mid-gesture, had a special quality. As Jean stared, she began to understand the silence, and the alarm on Andy's face.

Though his person was ugly, Albert was normally fastidious about cleanliness; his cheap clothing was neatly if clumsily patched, and he was always clean shaven. On this occasion he sported a straggling growth of black beard, and his shirt and trousers looked as if he had slept in them, not once but several times. As he stood blinking into the brightly lit room, his heavy shoulders hunched and his hands dangling, there was menace in his stance and in his squinting eyes.

If his appearance was alarming, his initial speech was even more so. Although Jean's French was poor, she knew the word he hurled at them like a missile.

"*Voleur!*"

A ripple of reaction ran through the staring crowd. Jean had time to wonder how personally some of the Trasteverites might take that accusation of "thief." The reputation of the district . . . Albert's voice rose to a shriek as he warmed to his subject.

"*Il a disparu. On l'a volé! Mon tresor, ma seule chose précieuse! Aujourd'hui,* today, when I go to eat the lunch—you steal—"

To Jean's horror, he began to cry. Though he continued to speak, the words were lost in his mammoth grief; the tears trickled down his face and collected in greasy puddles amid the folds of his vast brown cheeks. The crowd reacted as people usually do to an outburst of honest emotion; they turned their backs and resumed their conversations, a little more loudly than before.

Andy started toward the doorway. He reached his sobbing uninvited guest and slapped him on the back. It was a good hard slap, prompted by fury rather than camaraderie, but it stopped Albert's cries. He turned toward Andy, who began to speak, softly but urgently; and after a few moments Albert nodded and swabbed at his face with his sleeve. Andy took his arm and pulled him toward the table where the food was spread out. Jean relaxed. Andy had the situation well in hand. Albert could always be distracted by food. As she backed daintily away, she saw Ann making her way toward the table. The girl's face was set in an expression of controlled distaste, but she was obviously prepared to do her share in the dirty work.

Jean retreated, without shame. Albert in his normal state was bad enough; she had no desire to socialize with him while he was in his present state of mind. She joined a group of Italian students who were singing; one of them was strumming Andy's guitar. Over the melodious chords she could still hear the booming gutturals of Albert's voice. The sound of the syllables was unfamiliar; apparently he had relapsed into his native tongue. Andy admitted that he had forgotten most of the language which he had learned as a child, but the inattention of his audience never stopped Albert from talking.

For a while Jean forgot about the intruder. Then another flurry around the refreshment table caught her attention. Andy was no longer there, but José and Ted had joined Albert. After a moment Ann broke away and came hurrying toward Jean. She was flushed and distressed.

"What's the matter?" Jean asked.

"Oh, just Albert being Albert."

"What did he do, pinch you?"

"After a year in Rome I'm used to being pinched," Ann said. "That nasty little . . . If I were sure he's only ignorant and uncouth I wouldn't mind so much."

"I know what you mean. Can't the boys sort of edge him out of here?"

"The minute Andy left . . ." Ann was still preoccupied with her grievance.

"He's back," Jean said. "He's offering Albert more wine. I think he's trying to get him drunk."

Reluctantly, Ann turned.

"That won't work. Most people get more repulsive when they're drunk. Can you picture Albert?"

Ann was honestly distressed. She seemed close to tears, despite her caustic comments. Jean put her arm around the other girl.

"Let the boys handle him. Why should we be noble?" Ann produced a faint smile.

"They really are great—Ted and José, I mean. They both came rushing up when they saw I was having a hard time. If they hadn't—"

She broke off with a gasp as someone screamed.

It was only an overexcitable young lady who had misinterpreted the scene now transpiring. Whether Andy had planned it or not, Albert had definitely taken too much of something. He began to fold up, with Andy holding one arm and José the other. Carefully the two lowered him until he lay on his back on the floor. Even in unconsciousness Albert was not silent. He snored hideously.

"Out cold," Andy said, in the midst of a fascinated silence. "Somebody help me with him. Mike, Carlo—"

Michael put his sketch pad away.

"What did you do, slip him a Mickey?"

"I was thinking of it," Andy admitted. "He must have had a few drinks before he got here. He couldn't pass out on a couple of glasses of wine."

"Get him out of here, Andy," Ann said. She stared down at the prostrate form, her face a mask of disgust. "What a mess!"

Michael reached out to help, but Andy needed none. Stooping, he hoisted the limp body to his shoulder. The boy named Carlo followed him out. Jean gathered that Carlo had been elected to return Albert to the shabby room he called home.

"That young man is getting to be a problem," said José.

"A well-developed persecution complex," Ted agreed.

"But if someone robbed him . . ." Jean began.

"A delusion," José said. "The poor wretch has nothing worth stealing. Even his clothing is cheap, worn—"

"Perhaps he has lost his priceless collection of holy pictures," Ted said callously. "I thought I caught a reference to Saint Petronella. Whoever she was."

Jacqueline and Scoville joined the group in time to hear the last comment.

Scoville shook his head.

"I must say, this lad is an unprepossessing specimen. I remember his father, vaguely. Never amounted to much. . . . Why did you take up with him, after all these years, Ann?"

Andy, dusting his hands ostentatiously, came back into the room. His grin faded as he heard his father's question.

"He picked us up," he said, scowling. "And he's no weirder than some of your pals."

Scoville laughed and slapped his son on the back. Andy looked stoical, and the others, slightly embarrassed by this display of parental regard, pretended not to notice.

"That's the truth. Right on. I guess it runs in the family. Andy has a weakness for lame ducks. I remember that poor kid—"

"Why Petronella?" Ann said. "I never heard of a saint by that name."

"Rome is full of churches dedicated to saints nobody ever heard of," Andy said irritably.

"But the legends are interesting," Dana drawled. She leaned gracefully against the wall, and the neckline of her blouse slipped down another inch. One deep breath, Jean thought, and that blouse is going to go; and if she's wearing anything under it, I'll be a—

"You may sneer," José said. "But you must admit that many of these so-called legends have been substantiated by archaeology."

Dana shrugged. Four pairs of masculine eyes shifted hopefully, but were disappointed; she had calculated the shrug to a hair's breadth.

"José, darling, don't bring up the Vatican excavations again."

"But they prove my point." José turned to Scoville, who nodded knowledgeably. "Even to a skeptic, the ruins found under the basilica of St. Peter must be impressive. Legend said that Saint Peter was buried beneath the high altar; and behold, a cemetery was found. There are Christian tombs among them; they date from the period of Nero, when Peter was supposed to have been martyred. At the base of the altar, human bones were found—the bones of a man of strong physique and advanced age. But the skull was missing. And, since the sixteenth century, there has been in the church of St. John Lateran a reliquary containing the head of Saint Peter."

The argument wasn't new to Jean; they had fought it out, animatedly but good-naturedly, after their joint expedition to the excavations. It was evidently new to Jacqueline, though, and her reaction amused Jean; she was so intrigued she caught José by the arm.

"Is that true? I read something about the excavations, but I didn't know they had actually found the remains of Saint Peter!"

"Uh-uh," Andy warned. "Don't flip, my love. Not even the Vatican has come out with a definite statement on that. The bones were there, but there were a lot of bones—tombs and graves all over the place."

"But the bones of an elderly man . . . the missing skull . . ."

With her face animated and her green eyes shining, she looked almost as young as the students around her. Scoville beamed approvingly at Jacqueline, and his son said tolerantly,

"Look, Marian, this happens to be a particularly complicated problem in excavation. It would take me two days to give you a summary of the details. But José is cheating a little. For one thing, there's not a single inscription mentioning the name of Saint Peter. When the early pilgrims visited the tombs of the martyrs they scribbled prayers on the walls. There are such prayers at Bethlehem and Jerusalem, at St. Peter's shrine on the Via Ostia—but not on the walls under the basilica."

"The name is there, in the cryptic alphabet," said José.

Andy took himself by the hair and appeared to be trying to lift himself up off the ground.

"I knew you were going to say that! Don't say that! There is no cryptic alphabet! It's just another one of those nutty theories—"

"Andy," said his sister firmly.

Jacqueline, her eyes still fixed on Andy, plunged one hand into her purse and began to rummage. The others watched, fascinated, until the hand finally emerged with a pen and notebook.

"Give me some references," she ordered.

Grinning, Andy obliged.

"Talk about a busman's holiday," he remarked. "Don't take us too seriously, Marian. Basically, Ignatius and I agree."

"These nicknames of Andy's!" José complained. "They drive me insane. I do not mind being addressed by the name of the founder of my order, but I do not comprehend, Jacqueline, why he calls you 'Marian.'"

"I was afraid someone was going to remember that," Jacqueline said resignedly. "There is a charming musical comedy whose heroine has that name. She is a librarian.

Now—" she said quickly as Andy showed signs of being about to break into song, "tell me on what you both agree."

"On the basic factuality of legends," José said.

"The thing is," Andy explained, "when we talk about legends being confirmed by archaeology, we mean that the basic fact is confirmed. The details always turn out to be quite different from those in the story. And, sadly enough, the romantic, magical elements are the ones that vanish under close examination. There probably was a British chieftain named Arthur, or Artos, who lived in the sixth century; but the Round Table and the chivalry and the shining towers of Camelot are pure fiction. The bull-man called the Minotaur never roamed the passages of the palace of Knossos; and the Great Flood of Genesis was a petty local affair. That," said Andy, "is what historians do. They are killers of the dream, murderers of legend."

José laughed.

"You don't kill dreams so easily, my egotistical friend. Legends have a kind of truth which is independent of reason. A belief is a fact in itself; that is what you skeptics never admit."

Absently, Andy made an extremely rude Italian gesture toward his friend, who responded in kind before resuming.

"In fact, when the legends of the saints can be checked, a surprising number can be confirmed. The underground excavations Andy has been showing us are a case in point. Under the most ancient churches there are Roman houses. . . ."

"There are ancient Roman remains under every damn

building in the city," Michael said. "What would you expect to find? Egyptian pyramids?"

"Wait a minute, wait a minute," Jacqueline interrupted. "You keep talking about excavating under churches. How can they do that without destroying the church?"

"But this is Andy's specialty," Ted said. "Have you escaped his lectures? How did you manage to do that?"

Andy gave him a friendly shove.

"You dragged us through miles of your ancestral catacombs," he said. "And Jean showed us mosaics till the sight of a pile of gravel made me break out in hives. The Vatican picture galleries echoed to Michael's critical sneers, and Dana got her innings when we went through the classical collections." He turned to Jacqueline. "We're showing each other Rome," he explained. "Early Christian Rome is part of my specialty, so I'm taking the crowd through subterranean excavations. It is possible to dig without destroying the overlying structure, but it isn't easy."

"Interesting," Jacqueline admitted.

"Oh, we're all very earnest and hard-working," Michael said sarcastically. "And trying to get cultured. Personally, I find it uphill work. I don't dig this archaeology bit. Ann's tour was kind of interesting; I really go for Egyptian sculpture."

He smiled at Ann; and Ann, surprised and pleased, gave him a shy smile in return. Jean was so intrigued by this exchange that she lost track of the conversation momentarily. She returned to it in time to hear Andy inviting Jacqueline to join them on their tour next morning.

"We're going to San Clemente," he explained. "It's a

prize specimen; not just one subterranean level, but two. Three layers of construction. The present church was built in the twelfth century, on top of a fourth-century basilica which, in turn, stands on the walls of some Roman houses and a temple to Mithra."

"A Mithraeum?" said Scoville, his eyes narrowing.

"Oh, no, you don't," said his son.

"Don't what?"

"Horn in on my lecture tour. You're leaving for Sicily tomorrow."

"I see why you want me out of the way," Scoville said. "All that talk about finishing your report to the Fellowship Committee was a blind; you probably did it long ago. You just want to lecture without my critical eyes on you."

"I don't want you butting in," Andy said. "You can't keep quiet while somebody else talks about archaeology."

"Not when they make mistakes I can't keep quiet."

"I," said Andy, "never make mistakes. Tell you what. If you keep your mouth shut you can come along when we go to San Sebastiano. I made an appointment for the twenty-ninth."

"That's a deal."

"That gives you time to read up on the subject," Andy said, grinning.

"If I'm to be at the church at ten, I'd better get home," Jacqueline said. "Andy, it's been a lovely party."

Scoville left with her, claiming he had to hit the sack early if he wanted to catch his 6 A.M. train. Watching them leave side by side, Jean wondered. In the doorway Jacqueline turned, and Jean's pleasant speculations died. Jacqueline's face was not that of a woman who is headed toward a romantic tête-à-tête. She looked worried. Jean recalled her odd comments earlier that evening, and all at once, with an illogical certainty as strong as Jacqueline's, she knew the older woman was right. There was something wrong, some false note in the once harmonious relations of the group. It had been present all evening, under the seeming hilarity of the party. She had no more idea than Jacqueline what its source might be, but one thing was sure: Albert's grotesque behavior was part of the problem.

THREE

THE small sunken courtyard was paved with brick. The same warm reddish-brown material composed the facade of the church, with its unpretentious entrance portico supported on four small columns. The sun beat down onto the bricks; it was going to be a hot day.

They were there, all seven of them, plus Jacqueline Kirby. Most of them looked as if they wished they had stayed in bed. Michael was a study in sagging muscles and wrinkled cloth; he had propped himself up against one of the columns of the portico. Ann was wearing sunglasses, but when she took them off for a moment Jean saw stark purple circles under her eyes. A blue bandanna, tied in back of her head, confined her hair. Her dark jeans and shirt made her face look paler; her lipstick, carelessly applied, suggested a streak of orange paint.

Andy never looked tired; lack of sleep only stimulated

him. The casual dark clothing that made his sister look sexless and boyish only increased Andy's good looks.

Of all the group, the one who was most obviously hung over was Ted. He had all the symptoms: his eyes were bloodshot, his hands shook, and he winced visibly whenever a car out in the street blasted its horn. The sight of him made Jean's jaw drop. Ted seldom drank anything more potent than wine, and not much of that. She had never seen him drunk, and even with the obvious stigmata, which are considered so amusing by people who have never experienced them, Jean could hardly believe it if Dana had not confirmed her suspicion.

"You missed all the excitement, leaving so early," the English girl said in a gleeful whisper. "Ted was a panic. I mean, he was the life of the party. He was singing and reciting limericks in Hebrew and making passes at every girl in the room—"

"All of them?"

"Well, primarily me," Dana admitted, with a smirk that made Jean want to smack her face. "I've underestimated that lad. He's really something after he's loosened up a little."

Jean looked up and saw Ted watching them. He gave her a sickly smile and she glanced away.

"Do shut up," she said nastily. "I'd rather hear Andy lecture on his specialty than you on yours."

As Andy was the first to admit, he loved to talk, and he had inherited his father's gift for smooth, popular description. But this morning he was cutting the lecture short. The restlessness of his audience seemed to affect him. Even José, who was usually a courteous listener, finally called out,

"Andy, let's get inside, shall we? This quaint costume of mine is weighing me down."

"Right," Andy said. "I just wanted to say—ah, hell, look it up in the guidebook. And listen—anybody who wants to come back to our place and finish up the leftovers from last night is welcome. Just be back here at twelve. I'm not going to search that maze below for lost Sinners."

The group broke up and Jean, feeling somewhat fed up with her unkempt friends, crossed the courtyard to where Jacqueline stood demurely in a corner like a prim little wren in a crowd of starlings. Her feet, in neat white pumps, were placed at an angle of forty-five degrees; her auburn hair shone like a cap, with not a strand out of place; her ladylike silk print dress came down to the center of her knees. She was even wearing white gloves. The purse, of course, was prominent.

"Who are you trying to impress?" Jean asked.

"The elderly Italian lady with whom I am lunching. She happens to be a dear friend of the head of the university library where I am currently employed."

"You're a hypocrite," Jean said, remembering the sleek pants suit of the previous night and the general air of relaxation that had accompanied the change in costume.

"I merely adjust to my surroundings."

"Camouflage?"

"Protective coloring." Jacqueline's voice was unexpectedly hard. "Survival is a lot more difficult than you think, my friend." And then, as if she regretted her momentary lapse into cynicism, she added in a lighter tone, "The head librarian of the Classics Collection is retiring next year, and I may be in line for the job if I can prove I spent the summer studying the subject. I trust I need not remind you that the Institute library is one of the best in the world in that field."

"That must be why you're cultivating us," Jean said, with a grin. "Are you picking our brains?"

"Naturally," Jacqueline said, with an answering smile.

"You may regret that admission. We're all indefatigable lecturers."

They entered the church, and Jacqueline glanced appreciatively around its columned nave, with the brilliant mosaic of the apse at the far end.

"I'd rather hear you lecture about this than discuss classification with Lise. Go ahead, educate me. . . . What's the matter with Andy? He looks as if he's about to have a fit."

"He wants us to come. That must be the entrance to the underground area, over there."

"But I want to see this," Jacqueline complained.

Jean beamed.

"On behalf of my century, let me thank you. Mosaics are my thing, you know, and this is a particularly good one."

Instinctively they spoke in subdued voices. Though there was no service in progress, worshipers knelt at the various altars. Jacqueline lagged, deliberately.

"It's beautiful. And look at the frescoes in that chapel! Aren't they by Masaccio?"

"The attribution is disputed," Jean said, in mild surprise. "You have been doing your homework, haven't you?"

"I read my *Guida di Roma* last night," Jacqueline admitted. "The one put out by the Italian Automobile

Association is first-rate. I can't help it anymore, it's habit, after all these years, to look everything up. . . . Blast and curse Andy; what does he want now?"

"He wants us to come and see his pet ruins," Jean said, laughing. "This basilica is twelfth-century; Andy won't even look at anything later than the fourth. We'd better go; we can come back here later."

Andy was waiting for them at the entrance to a room which had been fitted up as an office. There were books and souvenirs for sale; Dana leaned over the ticket counter chatting with a very young, very handsome boy in the white robe of a Dominican. Jean went to the counter to buy her ticket, and overheard a snatch of conversation which explained some of Dana's fascination.

". . . it'll be the oldest of them in the city," said the soft Irish voice; then the priest looked up, smiled, and offered Jean her ticket.

As she stood waiting for Jacqueline to pay her hundred lire, Jean caught a glimpse of someone walking down the nave of the church. It was only a fleeting glimpse, but the shambling form was unpleasantly familiar. It wouldn't be unusual for Albert to track them down and add himself, uninvited, to the group. Hastily Jean trotted down the stairs to the first landing, where she was out of sight from the nave, and after a moment Jacqueline joined her. If she had seen Albert she didn't mention it, and Jean decided not to bring up the subject.

At the bottom of the long flight of stairs the modern world vanished. They stood in a vast dark place smelling of damp, and Jean had to look back at the well-lit staircase to assure herself that she had not been suddenly transported into another era.

A shadowy form materialized beside them.

"Boo," it said, in sepulchral tones.

Jean started.

"Damn it, Andy, that isn't funny."

"It's not funny, but it's appropriate," Jacqueline said. They still spoke in low tones; the atmosphere of the place was more suggestive of cemeteries than churches, but the inhibition was similar; there was a feeling that a loud voice might raise something better left undisturbed. Jacqueline added, "I'm completely confused. Where are we?"

"We're standing in what was once the narthex—the porch—of a basilica built in the fourth century A.D.; one of the first churches ever built. It wasn't until after Constantine legalized Christianity in the early fourth century that the Christians dared construct public places of worship. It's hard to picture how this place looked in its original state. There are walls now where columns stood originally; when they excavated this place, in the last century, they had to leave a lot of the fill in place, to keep the church up above from collapsing. The basilica above this is almost exactly on top of the fourth-century church, wall for wall."

Involuntarily both women glanced up at the dark ceiling, which now seemed to be pressing down on their heads.

"I hope they left plenty of nice solid dirt in place," Jean muttered. "You know, Andy, a person could get claustrophobia down here."

"There isn't much to see in this area," Andy admitted.

"Just a few moldy fragments of frescoes. When you're finished here, take those iron stairs down, and you'll drop back another three hundred years—back to the first century A.D. The walls you'll see down below were built to replace houses that burned in the great fire of Nero."

At some point in the next half hour Jean lost Jacqueline. That was one of Jacqueline's better qualities: you didn't have to talk to her, or be polite. Not only did she expect you to do your own thing, she was quite capable of going off and doing hers, without comment or explanation. The spell of the dark ruins was a melancholy, morbid charm, but it was hypnotic. Occasionally she encountered other shadowy wanderers; once she caught a glimpse of Ann's flaming hair. There were few other tourists; San Clemente was not on the regular route, and only specialists and people who had many weeks to spend in Rome found time for it.

Confusing as the fourth-century church was, it was a marvel of simplicity compared with the lowest level. Jean knew approximately what she was going to see there. As Andy had explained, there were essentially two buildings—or rather, parts of two buildings, for both had been only partially excavated. One of them was a private house, or palazzo, with rooms surrounding a large courtyard. The other structure was an apartment building, in the courtyard of which, eighteen hundred years earlier, a small temple of Mithra had been built.

The low vaulted ceiling suggested the roughly rounded roof of a cave, an impression which was reinforced by the damp atmosphere. The lighting was artfully dim, but it was enough to illumine the benches built along both the long walls, and the stone altar in the center of the floor.

Jean was examining the relief on the side of the altar when José joined her.

"A friendly face," he said, with relief. "I think I have been lost. This area is truly a maze."

"The level above is almost as bad." Jean indicated the relief, which showed a vigorous, youthful male figure in the act of stabbing an animal which it held by the horns. "I take it this is Mithra?"

"No doubt." José peered at the stone. "The youthful hero who slew the bull and, by the outpouring of its blood, gave immortality to mankind. An eastern cult . . . But you would know more about that than I."

"I don't know much either. Except that it was popular in the early centuries of the Christian era, and had some elements in common with Christianity."

"What elements?"

"Mithraism had a high ethical code, if I recall correctly. And the concept of sacrifice . . . Immortality through the shedding of blood . . ."

"The Blood is the Life," said José. His voice echoed oddly in the low-ceilinged chamber, and Jean glanced at him in surprise. His dark, chiseled face had an abstracted expression. "It is an old idea, is it not? It must go back beyond civilization, into the prehistoric time, when the ape-people died red the bones of their dead to restore to them the hue of life. . . . Brrr." He smiled; the flash of white teeth lightened the somber planes of his face. "I make myself morbid. This place is too dark; I am going up into the sunshine."

"I'll see you later."

Jean watched the tall black-robed figure move out through the narrow doorway; and she thought that his archaic costume suited the place. She was the one who was out of place here; the very walls seemed to reject her short skirt and bright flowered blouse, her sandaled feet and long, unbound hair.

She went out into the corridor, passing a fat lady and her balding husband, in order to investigate some of the rooms on that side. If the area had a plan, it eluded her completely. Rooms and corridors succeeded one another in a mazelike muddle. And all of it was empty. The neat tiled floors were dusty, and the walls had been stripped down to the naked brick. The emptiness was not just the absence of any accouterment of living, it was a positive force that pressed down on any creature daring enough to penetrate those chambers. Now and again Jean met other visitors, and passed them without speech; they all had the same blank, awed stare she felt on her own face.

Eventually she passed through a narrow doorway and found herself treading a path through a corridor walled in by rough, unexcavated heaps of rubble. She heard approaching footsteps long before she could identify the person who made them. Then she recognized Michael.

"Hey," Michael said. "It's you. . . . A few more minutes and I'd have started seeing ancient Roman ghosts. What a place!"

"What is it about the place? I've been in ruined buildings before. . . . Pompeii, the Acropolis, various digs . . . The only other place that oppressed me in this way was the catacombs."

"It's a dead place," Michael said. His eyes were so wide

she fancied she could see a rim of white all the way around the iris. "It's inimical to life."

"Getting psychic?" Jean asked jokingly.

Michael shrugged—or shivered, she wasn't sure which.

"Oh, crap," he said, in a more normal voice. "It's all calculated effect. The light, just dim enough to make your vision uncertain; the chilly dampness; the . . . listen."

In the silence Jean heard the sound to which he referred—a distant, rippling murmur that rose and fell like the voices of a far-off crowd.

"It's water," she ventured.

"An underground spring or stream. They had to dig a tunnel out to the main sewer to keep these rooms from being flooded. There's one room, back over on the other side of the palazzo, where water rushes through the wall and the overflow trickles out through holes into a channel. It's a small trickle. But if you stare at it too long, the sound of the water gets louder and louder, and you start thinking maybe it will burst out, through the wall, and you wonder whether you'd have time to make your way through all these corridors and get to the stairs before the flood caught you. . . ."

"My God, you're in a morbid mood." Jean peered at him through the gloom, and saw, with a stir of alarm, that he was perspiring, even in the chill air. "Michael, are you sick?"

"Sick in the head," said Michael, with an odd choked laugh. "They call it claustrophobia. Such a nice sterile name for a feeling that turns your guts inside out and makes your brain clang around in your skull like a bell in a belltower. . . ."

Jean reached out and caught his hands, which were groping for something to hang on to. He fell back against the wall, his eyes closed, breathing heavily. Jean didn't know what to do, except maintain the clasp that was numbing her fingers. After a few seconds Michael opened his eyes.

"That's better," he mumbled. "Company helps. But I think I'd better get out of here."

There was barely room for them to walk side by side. Jean kept pace with him; she sensed that he was exerting all his self-control to keep from breaking into a headlong panicky run.

"Is this new?" she asked.

"No. I spent two years in analysis, some time back."

"But we do this underground bit all the time! I remember now, when we went to the Callixtus catacomb you didn't say a word the whole time; we were kidding you about it. . . . And when Ted showed us the Jewish catacombs you acted funny, and you said you had the emperor of all hangovers. . . . Why didn't you tell us about your phobia?"

"It sounds so stupid," Michael said. His voice had a childish petulance that made Jean want to laugh, but she knew better than to do so. There might be a degree of masochism in Michael's behavior, but there was also a considerable amount of courage.

"It does not sound stupid," she said firmly. "A lot of people have a slight touch of claustrophobia; I have myself, but it's just enough to add a certain spice to these expeditions for me—the way you enjoy hearing a ghost story even more when the room is dark. But in its severe form the feeling must be awful. I don't think a doctor would approve of you pushing yourself this way."

"The only way I'll ever beat it is by pushing myself," said Michael. He sounded almost normal; only the painful grip of his hand betrayed his feelings. "Here we are. The stairs—freedom! Are you going to escort the baby up and out?"

"No," Jean said, stopping short. "You don't need an escort, and I—oh! Oh, my Lord—what's this? It's a grave, right on the wall—"

Michael laughed, more easily; her inadvertent alarm had been, by chance, the most tactful emotion she could have expressed.

"There are several graves. Enjoy yourself with the ghosts; I'll see you later."

He went up the steep modern iron staircase with more speed than caution, his long legs eating up the steps. When the echo of his steps had died away, the place seemed very quiet.

Jean turned to examine the graves. Cut into the perpendicular face of the wall, they were of the same type as those found in the catacombs. She knew she was reacting to Michael's nervousness, and with deliberate intent she made herself linger, trying to decide whether the scratches on the wall were only scratches, or a half-obliterated inscription. Illogically, the sound of footsteps approaching did not reassure her; she started nervously, and stared down the gloomy corridor as if she might see something. . . .

The something turned out to be Dana; which, Jean told herself, was not much better than nothing.

However, the other girl also seemed to be affected by the atmosphere. She greeted Jean with moderate enthusiasm.

"Thank God. I was beginning to feel as if I ought to be lying flat on my back, with my hands folded on my chest. Where does Andy find these jolly little places he takes us to?"

"It's funny you should feel that way."

"Why? Don't you find the place a bit uncanny?"

"Yes," Jean admitted. "But I should think this would be right up your alley. Aren't you used to digging up the dead past?"

"I've done some excavating. But on a normal dig you aren't working underground. Not unless you find tombs, and they're rare. . . . What's become of Andy? I haven't seen him since I came down to this level."

"I haven't either."

"I'm bored to tears and dying for a drink," Dana said petulantly. "This place is tedious. I don't know why Andy dragged us here. There's only one halfway decent thing, the ceiling stuccos on the pronaos of the temple. I rather liked them."

"I didn't see any stuccos. Just the benches and the altar."

"That room isn't the pronaos, it's the triclinium. The dining area," Dana added patronizingly. "Where they held the ritual meal. The pronaos is across the hall. You didn't see it? You must not have been looking at much."

"You must have paid more attention to Andy's lecture than I did."

"I cheated." Dana's sulky face relaxed. "I bought a guidebook. Look here, it has plans of all three of the levels on transparent paper, so you can see exactly where each section lies in respect to the one above and below."

"Hey, that's neat. I wish I'd had it before. I don't know where I've been."

"You can borrow it," Dana said. She yawned, brushing her mouth with the back of her hand. "You haven't run into Mike, have you? I promised I'd meet him here; but I guess he got tired of waiting."

"He went upstairs a few minutes before you came."

"Thanks."

She went up the stairs, undulating. With a comment that would have been represented in the old days of publishing by a dash and an exclamation point, Jean swung on her heel and marched back along the passage. It was injured dignity, not interest in the stuccos Dana had praised, that made her go that way, but when she reached the end of the passage she decided she might as well have a look at the stuccos. She realized then that Dana had not given her the guidebook, and she swore again, more emphatically. Surely, though, she could find her way back the way she had come.

The assumption turned out to be incorrect. After several turns, which seemed to her to be the reverse of the course she had originally followed, she found herself in a room she didn't remember having seen before. It was a fairly large room, approximately twenty feet square. Its floor was formed of buff-colored tiles, laid in a neat herring-bone pattern. There were small blocked-up openings which might have been windows once upon a time, but it was difficult to imagine that any normal human activity had ever been carried on here. The room was not only deserted, it looked as if it had never been occupied.

For several minutes she had been increasingly conscious of a sound. It was not a frightening noise, being, in fact, the murmur of water Michael had mentioned earlier. As she proceeded, through a narrow curved corridor, the sound increased in volume. There was a single door at the end of the corridor. Beyond, in the odd dusty light, she could see part of a brick wall. She went on, hoping to find a passage through.

In the doorway she stopped short. There was no other door. The passage by which she had come was the only entrance into the room. But it was not the finality of the fact that caused her to stop and drove the breath out of her lungs in an explosive cry of horror.

Unlike the other, this room was occupied—but not, she thought, by any living thing. The man who lay face down on the floor, in a sickening puddle of red, was not alive. Nothing could bleed that much and still be alive.

When the sprawled body moved, she tried to scream, and failed; she had forgotten to breathe in, after the first shocked exhalation. Then she forgot about screaming. The eyes in the ashen face were glazed, but they caught her own eyes with a concentrated intensity of demand that made her forget her feelings. Jean knelt down on the dreadful floor and reached out to support the man's hanging head.

She had recognized Albert even before she saw his face, from the patched clothing and plump body. She was never sure afterward whether he knew her or not; but he sensed another presence, and his desire to communicate was so strong it drove his fading will to an effort she would have believed impossible.

He tried to speak. She saw his mouth move and concentrated on its shape because she could not, would not, look at the gaping gash below. He had nothing left to speak with, not even breath. The fading eyes closed. Then they opened again on a new blaze of will, and one stained finger moved.

Later, trying desperately to find some small redeeming feature in the situation, Jean was glad that Albert's failing mind missed the obvious source of writing material. His finger left no bloody trail; it merely scratched a darker pattern through the dust of the floor, and if she had not seen the shapes forming, she would never have recognized them. Caught in the hypnotic pull of the dying man's concentration, she followed the slow, painful strokes with pent breath.

Then the hand clenched in a sudden spasm. The head dropped heavily onto Jean's supporting hands. Gently she lowered it to the floor and stared with dilating eyes at her reddened hands, and the ugly streaks on her knees and skirt. She rose jerkily to her feet. Softly in the background, like a musical accompaniment, she could still hear the rippling murmur of running water.

FOUR

JEAN was under the mistaken impression that she was thinking quite rationally. She began to scream—not in panic, she assured herself, but simply as a means of procuring help. She couldn't run away, because that would mean leaving . . . him. It? The living entity has gender; the dead are neuter. She wondered whether she had chanced on some deep philosophic truth, or whether the difference only mirrored a meaningless distinction taken over from a language in which all nouns have gender. The designations made no sense; why should a French pen be feminine, and a pencil masculine?

Her breath gave out, and she stopped screaming. In the silence she heard footsteps. They were approaching rapidly, almost at a run. Someone had heard her. Her knees went weak with relief and she knew, then, how close she had come to hysterics. With a long, childish wail of distress and welcome, she stumbled forward and threw herself into Jacqueline Kirby's arms.

"What is the matter with—" The voice, sharp with concern, broke off in a gasp as Jacqueline saw. There was a moment of absolute silence; Jacqueline's store of expletives was evidently inadequate for the occasion.

"All right," she said, after a moment. "Stop that bawling, Jean. Stop it right now, do you hear me?"

Without waiting for a response she pulled herself away from Jean and began fumbling in her purse. Her voice, deliberately harsh and unsympathetic, had quieted Jean somewhat, but she was still too distressed to see what Jacqueline was doing until an exquisite agony invaded her nostrils and turned the interior of her head to fire.

"Oh, God, that hurt!" she moaned, wiping streaming eyes. "Smelling salts! You sadistic, mean—"

"That's better." Jacqueline restored the bottle to her purse. "Someone has to go for help, Jean. I don't think anyone else heard you."

Pushing the tangled hair back from her eyes, Jean

looked at her companion and saw another facet of Jacqueline's complex personality. Her face was ashen and as hard as her voice. Its strength was reassuring, and a little frightening.

"I didn't do it," Jean said, gulping.

"For God's sake, don't say that to anyone else!" Jacqueline's hard-won control broke momentarily. The green eyes turned glassy with a new fear. "Don't volunteer anything. Oh, God—you aren't in any state to be left alone, are you?"

"I think," said Jean, swallowing strenuously, "I think I'm going to be sick."

"Get it over with, then," Jacqueline said brutally. She fumbled in the purse and eventually produced an object that made Jean's eyes widen, even in her queasy state. It looked like—it was—a policeman's whistle.

The succeeding interval was unpleasant enough to occupy Jean's entire attention. She was vaguely aware of piercing blasts from the whistle, and of firm hands that held her shoulders while she suffered. When she had recovered sufficiently to notice what was going on, the room seemed to be filled with people. The first one she saw was Andy; his fiery mop of hair stood out in the dusty room, and it looked even brighter against the greenish pallor of his face. Someone was kneeling by the body, hiding all of it except the outstretched legs. No—there were two people kneeling, both wearing the long ecclesiastical robe. One white and one black; José, and one of the Dominican fathers. They rose, and as they stood side by side they resembled symbolic representations of good and evil, hieratic, in their medieval robes. The young

Dominican was as unmistakably Irish as José was Latin; but the two faces had a peculiar identity of expression. They exchanged glances, and José nodded slightly.

"I'll have to be calling the police, then," said the soft, inflexible Irish voice.

As she gazed around the room, Jean thought that surely no criminal investigation had been carried on in more outré surroundings. The triclinium of the temple of Mithra had seen strange rites in its time, but nothing quite like this.

José had suggested the temple room, with its rows of built-in benches, as the least uncomfortable place in which the witnesses might wait. There was really no other suitable room in either of the two lower levels, and the upper church, with its crowd of local worshipers, was obviously unsuitable. So they were herded one by one into the ancient sacred place as the priests located them— the seven, and Jacqueline, and half a dozen miscellaneous and distracted tourists. Dana and Michael were the last to be found, in a remote corner of the fourth-century church. Nobody asked them what they had been doing there, but as they came into the room Andy laughed, suddenly and sardonically.

"Number six and number seven," he said. "Fellow Sinners, it appears that the name was a meaningful inspiration after all."

"If you mean what I think you mean, you are jumping to conclusions," Ted said. He was sitting beside Ann, who looked terrible. Her freckles stood out like dots made with the blunted end of a lipstick. Ted went on, "You don't know how he was killed. It might have been an accident."

"His throat was cut," Jean said. The sound of her own voice made her jump.

"Jesus, Mary, and Joseph," muttered Michael. "Did you—" He looked at Jean, who was sitting between Jacqueline and an elderly American lady.

"Yes, I found him. And if you don't mind, I'd rather not describe it. I'll have to tell the police when they arrive. . . ."

"Yes, and where are your precious fuzz?" Dana demanded. "I've been sitting on this damned stone slab so long . . ."

She completed the sentence with a picturesque if unoriginal metaphor that made the gray-haired lady gasp. One of the other strangers, a bearded youth with bare feet and a knapsack on his back, beamed admiringly. Two other women looked like schoolteachers. One of them said drily,

"I agree with the sentiment, if not the exact words. Have the police been summoned? There were two of them lounging about outside when we came in—the ones who wear those gaudy uniforms, with the cocked hats and the swords."

"*Caribinieri*," Andy said. He was looking sick and strained, but he could never resist explaining things. "A case of—a case like this wouldn't come under their jurisdiction. There are three different kinds of cops here. The *caribinieri* are a military force, though they can pursue and apprehend civilian-type crooks. The city police—the *polizia municipale*—are the ones you see directing traffic and giving tickets. I think we'll be questioned by the third group, the *agenti* of the Commissario di Pubblico

Sicurezza. Each district of Rome has its own local subdivision—"

"I do not see why we should be questioned." The speaker was a stout, balding man who was accompanied by his stout wife. Jean couldn't place his accent; he wasn't American or British. "I intend to complain. I fail to see why we have been detained."

"I agree," snapped one of the teachers. "I don't even know what has happened."

"A man is dead," Jacqueline said. It was the first time she had spoken, and all of them turned to look at her. "He died violently. We must expect to be detained. That is normal procedure in any civilized country."

She had reverted to her prim librarian role, with her glasses firmly in place and her gloved hands folded over the pregnant bulge of the purse. For Jean, the purse had assumed a magical aura; from its depths, only today, had come the smelling salts, the whistle, a huge man's (man's?) handkerchief with which to mop her wet face, and a mysterious little white pill. Jean suspected the pill was only aspirin. Jacqueline was not the type to carry tranquilizers. But its psychological effect had been excellent. She felt numb, but calm.

"But I don't know the man!" one of the other tourists protested. "Why drag us into this?"

"That's up to the police, not us," Jacqueline said. "If you don't know the victim you probably won't be detained for long. So what are you worrying about?"

"Very true."

Occupied with their bickering, they had not observed the unobtrusive approach of the newcomer. As they saw him, a silence of awesome proportions fell on the group. It was broken by Dana.

"Well," she said softly. "I have to admit it was worth waiting for."

The man standing in the doorway was obviously the police official they had been expecting. He was, just as obviously, the kind of Roman gentleman female visitors dream of meeting but seldom do.

His dark hair shone, thick and soft, in the dim light. The two wings of silver lifting from his temples were almost too perfect; they looked as if they had been sprayed on. Jean, who was sitting near the door, saw his face in profile, and the sharp, delicate features reminded her of an antique portrait head from ancient Rome. The modeling of nose and chin and cheekbone was so precise they might have been cut from marble; except for his superbly tailored modern clothing, the man could have stepped out of the procession carved on Augustus' Altar of Peace.

After making a leisurely survey of the group seated on the right-hand benches, he turned his head to the left, and Jean's glance met his wide-set dark eyes. A little shock ran through her. The young Octavian, planning his rise to imperial power, might have had eyes like those—cool, appraising, frighteningly intelligent.

The eyes moved over them, one by one.

"I am di Cavallo. A humble *agente* of the Questura."

Andy, who had been slumped wearily against the wall, sat up with a start.

"Aren't you Lieutenant di Cavallo?"

"That is my official title. I do not recall having had the honor of your acquaintance. . . ."

Andy smiled faintly. There was a curious gleam in his eyes as he measured the other man.

"You have a certain reputation, Lieutenant." He turned to the others. "We're honored, ladies and gentlemen. Normally a simple *agente,* or maybe a noncom, is in charge of criminal investigations. I didn't expect an officer of the lieutenant's distinction."

Di Cavallo was unmoved by the flattery.

"Your knowledge of our governmental procedures is admirable, young man. Now, if you have finished displaying that knowledge, perhaps I may proceed? Thank you. . . ." He turned to Jacqueline, clearly approving her poised look and respectable appearance. "I am told, signora, by Father Finnegan, that you appear to be acquainted with the dead man, and also with several of these witnesses. Can you tell me what happened?"

In a few sentences Jacqueline identified Albert and explained his relationship to the other members of the group, whom she introduced. When she had finished her brief account the lieutenant nodded.

"The papers in the wallet of the dead man identify him as you have said. You, you, you two—" Unerringly he selected the casual tourists. "You have never met this Albert Gébara? Then you may leave. Please give your names and your local addresses to the police officer in the vestibule. Thank you."

When the outsiders were gone there was a noticeable change in the atmosphere. Di Cavallo sat down in one of the vacated places and reached into the breast pocket of his jacket. Taking out a gold cigarette case which looked too flat to hold anything thicker than a toothpick, he offered it to the group at large before taking one himself. Jean felt fairly certain that detecting was not di Cavallo's sole source of income. Surely, if he were a dishonest cop, he wouldn't display his opulence so openly. He must come from a wealthy family.

"Lieutenant," Ted began, "are you not being rather casual about those others? Just because they say they do not know the murdered man—"

"Murdered?" Di Cavallo raised his eyes from the tip of his cigarette and exhaled a cloud of fragrant smoke. "Why do you think this is a case of murder?"

The silence vibrated. Finally José said drily,

"The man's throat was cut, Lieutenant. That could hardly be an accident."

The lieutenant's eyes settled on the priest, and met their match. For a moment the two pairs of dark eyes locked. Then di Cavallo grinned.

"Padre Ximenez? I would have recognized the Jesuit even without the cassock. You are quite right, Father. It is not often that a man slips so badly while shaving, and a man does not shave without water, soap, and a mirror, does he? No, we can certainly dismiss the idea of accident. But there is another category of violent death."

"Suicide!" Dana was never ingenuous; the exclamation was designed to catch the lieutenant's eye. It succeeded. The eye lingered.

"That is correct, signorina. What do you know of this matter?"

Dana shrugged prettily.

"Fortunately, I wasn't the one to find the body."

"Fortunately indeed. It was not a nice sight."

"That wasn't what I meant," said Dana. Her eyes flickered. "In England . . . But you said this wasn't a case of murder."

"I have not yet said what it is a case of," said di Cavallo, handling the complicated English sentence with complete aplomb. "In England, you were about to say . . ."

"Oh, well." Dana shrugged again, bringing all kinds of useful muscles into play. "In English detective stories the one who finds the body is always a prime suspect. But as you said—"

Outrage overcame Jean's exhaustion, and she sat upright, glaring.

"Of all the—"

Her voice clashed with, and was overruled by, di Cavallo's voice.

"As I said, it does not seem to be a case of murder." He shrugged; the exquisite gesture made Dana's shrug seem crude. "I am violating regulations by saying this much; we have not yet completed our investigations. But this is an unusual case. We like to extend courtesy to our foreign visitors; we realize that our system of law is alien to the Anglo-Saxon, and that includes, I believe, most of you. So I will tell you, in confidence, that we have found the weapon under the body of the dead man. It is a common sort of knife, a kitchen knife, which may be purchased in any store here. And the nature of the wound bears out the assumption of suicide. It only remains, then, to find a reason why this unfortunate young man may have wished to end his life."

"He was crazy," Mike said.

All eyes focused on him where he sat huddled in a

corner. His knees were drawn up and his elbows rested on his knees; the pose was almost the classic embryonic position of withdrawal. Remembering his confession, Jean felt sorry for him—until she remembered where he and Dana had been found.

"He really was crazy," Michael repeated. "Everybody knows how he's been acting lately."

"Mike is right," Andy said. "Look, Lieutenant, it isn't as if the poor devil was a good friend of ours. We didn't know anything about his private life. He more or less butted into our group—I mean, he invited himself—"

"I know the English idiom," di Cavallo said stiffly.

"What? Oh . . . sure. What I was going to say was, even a casual acquaintance could tell he was mentally disturbed. And there was a change for the worse in the last few days. Wasn't there?"

His appeal to the group produced a murmur of agreement.

"Andy is correct," José said. "Albert was always peculiar, and lately he had become even more peculiar. You may not consider us good judges of normal behavior, Lieutenant; but perhaps you will accept Mrs. Kirby's opinion."

"Ah." Di Cavallo settled back, crossing his legs. "Mrs. Kirby, yes. Signora, you are an official of the Institute of Art and Archaeology?"

"No, I'm only a visiting librarian—a friend of Frau Hilman, who is librarian at the Institute. I'm not an expert on psychiatry, either, but I agree with my friends here that Albert was decidedly odd."

Clearly di Cavallo approved of Jacqueline; his eagle eye

softened whenever he looked at her. He nodded agreeably.

"In what specific way was he odd, signora?"

"Lieutenant," Ann said softly. "I'm sorry to interrupt, but Jean—she's the one who found him—it was a terrible experience for her, and she doesn't look at all well. Can't we take her home?"

For the second time that day Jean felt the full focus of di Cavallo's unnerving stare. She knew she must look as pale and pathetic as she felt, and the lieutenant's expression was properly sympathetic. But it didn't deceive Jean for a moment. Neither her youthful pathos nor Dana's sultry looks would have the slightest effect on this man.

"But of course," di Cavallo said. "If the young lady will first tell me—"

Ann got to her feet.

"She's in no condition to tell you anything. You know where to find us, we aren't going anywhere. Can't you question her later?"

"But there isn't anything to tell," Jean said. "I just walked into the room and there he was. I went to him, and knelt down; I thought perhaps I could help him. I didn't see the—the wound, then, not until he raised his head—"

Di Cavallo sucked his breath in sharply through his teeth.

"You are telling me, signorina, that the man was not dead when you found him?"

The suave manner was gone; voice and face were sharp with newly aroused suspicion. Jean realized that the others were staring at her with the same startled incredulity.

"He was dying, but not . . ." Jean turned to Jacqueline.

"You saw him. . . . No, you didn't come till after. . . . But he was alive! Just barely. I know it sounds incredible, but—"

"Not impossible," José's cool voice broke in. "There have been cases of fatally injured men who lived for—"

"Very well, Father, very well," di Cavallo interrupted. "Until I speak with the police surgeon, such speculation is irrelevant. Now, signorina. He raised his head. Did he speak, then?"

"No." Jean remembered that horrible voiceless whistle of breath, and a shudder ran through her. "He tried to, but he . . . He wrote something, though. On the floor, with his finger."

The general incredulity was so thick Jean could almost feel it. Di Cavallo continued to stare, but there was now more impatience than suspicion in his face. Apparently he took her for one of those suggestible witnesses who invent dramatic details after the fact.

"I saw the room, signorina. There was, I assure you, no last message scrawled in the dying man's blood."

"It wasn't scrawled in blood," Jean snapped. "He just scratched it in the dust. It was probably obliterated when he fell forward."

"Very well." Di Cavallo sighed. "And what were the man's dying words?"

"Not words. Not even one word." Jean looked wildly at the faces of her friends, and found them pitying, amused, protesting—and all unbelieving. "I tell you, he wrote it! The number seven!"

The room was almost dark when Jean woke up from a nap

she had had no intention of taking. Sitting up too suddenly, she clutched her spinning head and tried to orient herself. Slowly, memory returned. She was in Jacqueline's apartment, and apparently Jacqueline had slipped her a Mickey in that ritual cup of tea. She might have known that even Jacqueline wasn't old enough to really believe in the restorative properties of a nice hot cup of tea. . . .

Something was in the room with her. She could hear it breathing. After a long, horrible moment, she identified the lump at the foot of the bed as the sleeping poodle. Jean crept out of bed without rousing the animal; it looked so comfortable she couldn't bring herself to disturb it.

She located her hostess on the balcony off the *salone*. The railings were screened by thick masses of blue-flowered plumbago and the trailing greenery of ivy geraniums, pink and white and salmon-colored. Wearing shorts and a sleeveless blouse, Jacqueline was seated at a small table reading a book. She put the book down and greeted Jean coolly.

"How do you feel?"

"Groggy." Yawning, Jean dropped into a chair and propped her chin on her hands. "What did you give me?"

"A mild sedative."

"Mild!"

It was still daylight, but the sky to the east was beginning to darken. The evening breeze felt good after the airless bedroom; it lifted Jean's hair from her forehead, and she turned her face to it gratefully. Through the flowered greenery she could see the blue sparkle of the pool below.

"Corruption," she said dreamily.

"What?"

"Money corrupts. I wish somebody would try to corrupt me. I could learn to like living this way."

"So enjoy it while you're here. Would you like something to eat?"

With an effort Jean roused herself from the pleasant lethargy induced by the seductive air and the setting. "You've done enough. Not that I don't appreciate it, but I can't let you coddle me any longer. I'm going home."

"I'm not offering to serve you pheasant under glass on a tray in bed," Jacqueline said drily. "Prosciutto and rolls are what I had in mind. Your stomach is completely empty, and if you leave now you'll just pass out on the street somewhere. That doesn't make much sense, does it?"

She sounded as grouchy as an arthritic old lady, and Jean stared at her in surprise.

"You don't have to do this for me," she said stiffly.

"What else could I have done? You were in no state to be alone."

"Ann wanted me to come home with her and Andy."

"Yes, and your whole blasted club would have gone along, and sat there yelling and talking and rehashing the whole business. Seven Sinners, indeed! You're a bunch of irresponsible kids, every one of you."

"You really didn't want me to come here, did you?"

"No."

"Then why—"

Jacqueline sighed. She turned slightly in her chair and stretched her legs out. They were, Jean noticed, very good legs.

"I'm sorry, Jean, I shouldn't have said that. Don't take my meanness personally; I really like all of you mutts, even if you do exasperate me. It's just a personal foible. . . . Let's have a sandwich, and then you can go home. I'll wash my hands of the lot of you, with pleasure."

Her voice was light, and Jean knew her mood had improved. They brought their impromptu meal out onto the balcony; it was almost too beautiful to be real, with the sky slowly darkening to the precise, gleaming blue that appears in the starry vaults of the medieval church mosaics, and the perfumed breeze blowing through the heavy flower clusters. Jean found she was ravenous. Unashamedly she polished off every scrap of food on the table, and accepted a second helping.

"Every time I come here I eat like a glutton," she said apologetically. "You've been awfully nice. I really do appreciate it."

Jacqueline made a face.

"For God's sake don't use that word. Damning with faint praise . . . Nice, indeed."

"No, really," Jean persisted. "You're nice to put up with us. I suppose we seem pretty juvenile to you. What do you really think of us?"

Jacqueline considered the question.

"The Seven Sinners," she said, with a faint smile. "I guess the thing that strikes me is your mixture of erudition and naïveté. You're a bright lot, you know—collectively and individually. But you are very . . . young. I have to say that," she added, her smile widening. "If I praised your wisdom, the inner council of the over-thirty crowd might hear about it and I might mysteriously disappear some dark night. No remains would ever be found; only a terrified peasant would babble of flaring torches in a remote grove, where white-robed figures met in judgment over a traitor."

Jean laughed.

"Not bad. You ought to write thrillers."

"I've read too many of them," Jacqueline admitted. "When I started out, I worked in a small-town library where business was slow. Detective stories are among the few types of literature you can pick up and put down a dozen times per day." She took a sip of her wine—a beverage that, in Rome, accompanies the smallest snack. "And, in the last few hours, this has become a thriller. This life of yours."

"How true. Jacqueline . . . Do you honestly think Albert was the suicidal type?"

Silence followed the question. It was dark now; Jean saw her companion only as a featureless outline in the shadows. Finally Jacqueline said,

"Is there a suicidal type?"

"Don't quibble," Jean said. "Of course there isn't; I've had some experience along those lines myself; who hasn't? But I've never known any suicide, successful or unsuccessful, who acted like Albert."

"I keep forgetting what it was like to be twenty," Jacqueline said musingly. "And I gather it's worse these days. . . . How many suicides have you known?"

"Only one. And it turned out she was on acid. But I've heard a lot of people talk."

"God, yes. Of course you have. . . . All right, Jean, if you really want to go into this. Do you think Albert was taking any kind of drug?"

"No. No, I don't. You can tell."

"I know. Do I know. . . . You find me a parent who can't recite the symptoms of everything from hash to speed and I'll show you a stupid parent. . . . The autopsy will answer that question finally, but I think you're correct. Albert wasn't on anything. So?"

Jean made a despairing gesture.

"So . . . It's hard to express it. Albert was crazy, sure. But one thing he had, he had a very high opinion of Albert. Whether he was crazy or not . . . whether his theories were weird or not . . . he didn't know they were weird. He thought he was God's gift to the heathen world. All right, maybe I don't know enough about mental illness. Maybe he flipped. Maybe he went from a manic state to a depressive state, and realized that his pretensions were all lies, that he was an ugly, repulsive—"

Her voice broke. For a few seconds the silence was complete. Then Jacqueline's disembodied voice said,

"Epitaph for Albert . . . You have a rather nice mind yourself, child. Also you have had too much wine after a hard day. Make yourself another sandwich and listen while I agree with you. This business bothers me. It has bothered me all day. But, like yourself, I don't have any logical reason for being bothered."

The sound cut through her voice like a buzz saw; both of them jumped.

"Blast that doorbell," Jacqueline muttered. "It has the ugliest sound. . . . Stay here. I'll answer it."

By the time Jacqueline had reached the elevator door, switching on lights as she went, Jean had recovered herself. In the glow from the *salone* she calmly made herself another sandwich. She was chewing on it—the hard Italian rolls made mastication a real exercise—when Jacqueline returned with the man who had rung the doorbell. The sight of him was not cheering to Jean, but she couldn't help being amused at Jacqueline's expression. It was, as the old romances used to say, a study.

"Signorina." Di Cavallo made a bow so punctilious it looked like a joke. "You are feeling better now?"

Jean nodded and smiled. She couldn't speak; her mouth was full.

At Jacqueline's invitation the lieutenant sat down and accepted a glass of wine. He sighed loudly.

"How lovely it is, here in the darkness. And how lovely it would be to forget all unpleasant things. Alas, I must not allow myself, or you, that indulgence."

"What have you found out?" Jacqueline asked.

Di Cavallo sipped his wine.

"The case seems obvious. I now tie up the loose ends."

"Suicide?"

Di Cavallo nodded. He reached for the briefcase which all proper European businessmen, of all professions, habitually carry.

"Be so good to look at this," he said, taking out a sheaf of papers and handing them to Jacqueline.

Jacqueline shifted her chair so that she was sitting in the shaft of light from the *salone.* She peered nearsightedly at the papers.

"I can't see a thing," she muttered. "What did I do with my glasses?"

"They're on top of your head," Jean said, watching her

curiously. When Jacqueline acted disorganized and incoherent she was usually up to something.

"How ridiculous. What would they be—" Her groping hand found the glasses. Giving Jean a hard stare, she perched them on the end of her nose and began to read.

She read for some time, in silence. Her face was a studied blank, giving nothing away. After a time she glanced inquiringly at the lieutenant and then handed the papers to Jean.

The papers were Albert's notes. They were covered with writing in French, Arabic—and, surprisingly, in Latin. Not so surprising, though, Jean thought, as she leafed through the sheets. Albert's sources dated from the early Christian era, so naturally most of them would be written in Latin. But . . .

"But," she said slowly, "this is gibberish. None of it makes any sense."

"You understand the languages, signorina?"

"Yes, I read Latin and French, though I don't speak them. But it would be obvious, even with a slight command of the languages. All of it seems to be either prayers or . . . well . . . blasphemies. The names of saints, over and over . . . 'Santa Cecilia, *ora pro me*—Saint Cecilia, pray for me. Saint Christopher, pray for me. . . .' And this part seems to be a series of epithets, directed at the Pope."

"Yes, yes," di Cavallo said impatiently. "The work is that of a person whose religious views are eccentric, to say the least. What I wish to know is—are these papers as worthless as they seem to be?"

"They're not only mad, they're meaningless," Jean said, handing the papers back to di Cavallo. "Have you shown them to Andy Scoville? He knows more about the subject than I do."

"I have talked with him. He agrees."

"Is this all?" Jacqueline asked "All you found in his room?"

"All, yes. A few shabby clothes, books . . . letters from his mother . . ."

"His mother," Jean repeated stupidly.

"He had a mother, yes; it is not unusual." Di Cavallo studied her without sympathy or prejudice. "Signorina, it is all very sad, no doubt; but the world is full of tragedies, they occur every thirty seconds and many of them are sadder far than this loss of a very disturbed young man who might have injured some innocent person eventually if he had not had the kindness to remove himself first."

"You are sure?" Jacqueline's voice sounded odd, and di Cavallo peered at her through the shrouding darkness.

"Very little in this world is sure, Signora Kirby—as I think you, like myself, have learned through painful experience. But I am as sure as I am ever sure. . . . There are only a few loose ends. For example, this story of a theft."

"Who told you about that?"

"Padre Ximenez. He disapproves of me, as I do of him, but we respect one another. He pointed out to me that the accusation of theft must have been directed at one of your small group of friends, since Gébara knew none of the other guests."

"Yes, but that didn't mean anything. Nobody stole anything from Albert. He didn't have anything worth stealing."

"So one might conclude from the poverty of his belongings. Your friends agree that he never mentioned any particular treasure before last night. . . . The Seven Sinners," di Cavallo said musingly. "Very quaint . . . You did say, signorina, that the symbol written by the dying man was the number seven?"

For a second, Jean's breath stopped. Then she recovered herself.

"Would it be contempt of court or something if I said 'damn you,' Lieutenant?"

"It would only be very rude," said di Cavallo calmly.

"Yes, I did see him write that, and I stick to my story. But if this is suicide, the Seven Sinners can't have anything to do with Albert's dying message."

"I cannot see how," di Cavallo agreed. "If this were not so obvious a case—if there were any suspicion of foul play . . . Even then, I cannot see that there is a clue in that number. Because in a group of seven, any one might be number seven. You did not have numbers, did you, like the secret gangs in the old romances?"

"Of course not. We didn't even have an official name, it was just Andy's fooling."

"Well, then, we will never know. And it does not greatly matter. . . . Ladies, I think that is all. You are staying here tonight, Miss Suttman?"

"No, I'm going home. I've imposed on Mrs. Kirby long enough."

"Ah? Then I will be happy to take you home, if you are ready to go now."

"Well . . . thanks."

Jacqueline said nothing. She preceded them to the door, and Jean was gratified to note that di Cavallo shared the weaknesses of lesser men. His appraisal of Jacqueline's legs was leisurely, expert, and approving.

The lieutenant's car was an official vehicle, complete with driver. After asking directions, di Cavallo was silent until they reached Jean's apartment building. To her surprise and unexpressed alarm, he got out with her. He saw the alarm; there was amusement in his face as he condescended to explain.

"The other young woman—Miss Dana—also lives in this building, I believe. I wish to speak to her."

"She may not be in," Jean said, as they entered the building. "Dana leads an active social life."

"Yes, I would think she might," said the lieutenant gravely. "I wonder why, since your friend lives here with you, it was left to Mrs. Kirby to take you home today, after your bad experience."

"Dana doesn't live with me, she just has a room in the same building. We aren't exactly . . . I mean, we are friends, but not—"

"I think I understand."

"I wish I thought you did," muttered Jean. "What do you want to see her about?"

"Only to tie up the—"

"Loose ends. All right, ask a stupid question and you get a stupid . . . Sorry, I didn't mean that," she added quickly.

When they reached the third floor di Cavallo knocked on Dana's door. Jean hovered, unashamedly curious. She expected di Cavallo to order her away, but he did not, and when it became apparent that Dana was not at home, she suggested, "Maybe I could help you. What was it you were going to ask Dana?"

"I only wish to ascertain where each person was at the time of the tragedy. It is part of the routine."

"An alibi." Jean considered this. "You didn't ask me."

"But signorina," said di Cavallo silkily, "I know where you were when the man died. You were kneeling by his side. Is that not correct?"

FIVE

A S IT goes from the Piazza Barberini to the Porta Pinciana, the Via Veneto curves and climbs. Jean was trying to hurry because she was late, but she found it hard going. By the time she reached Doney's, at the far end of the street, she was limping perceptibly.

Jacqueline was already there, at one of the sidewalk tables under the blue-and-white awning. Her blue linen suit matched the blue of the awning and turned her eyes aquamarine. She was knitting busily. The wool was a lovely shade of blue, a bit darker than her suit, but it had a slightly battered look and Jacqueline scowled at it over the tops of her glasses, which rested precariously on the end of her nose. She looked up as Jean approached, and the scowl deepened into a look of concern.

"What happened to you?"

"Have you been waiting long?" Jean dropped into a chair.

"No, I was late myself. But what—"

"If I'd known you were going to be late I wouldn't have hurled myself under a taxi. Some less drastic excuse would have done just as well."

"You're kidding."

"Well, I didn't actually jump," Jean said. She stretched out her legs and inspected her scraped knees. "I was pushed."

Jacqueline bundled up her knitting with a carelessness that explained its dilapidated condition, and put it into the purse. She took out the box of Band-Aids and a small bottle.

"Oh, no." Apprehensively, Jean recognized the red liquid in the bottle. "Jacqueline, you are too much. Don't tell me you always carry . . . You can't do that here!"

Ignoring Jean's wails and the fascinated stare of the waiter, Jacqueline administered first aid as calmly as if she had been alone with her patient. The damage was extensive. When Jacqueline had slapped a series of bandages across each knee she put her materials back in the purse, glared at the waiter, who tried to look as if he were somewhere else, and inquired, "Are you all right?"

"Oh, sure. It isn't the first time some idiot has pushed me off the curb. Only this time . . . Well, I was lucky the taxi driver had good reflexes."

She spoke lightly, but the memory would not leave her in a hurry—the sick knowledge of her own helplessness as she looked up and saw the shining chrome of the grill bearing down on her.

"Anyway," she added, "I'd have gotten here if I had to crawl. It isn't every day I'm invited to lunch on the glamorous Via Veneto. We don't hang out here, it's too expensive."

"It's a tourist trap and an affront to the laboring masses," Jacqueline agreed placidly. She took the knitting out of her purse, studied it dubiously, shrugged, and began to knit.

"What is it?" Jean asked. "I don't want to sound nosy, but I can't see you as a doting grandmother, somehow."

"It's supposed to be a sweater," Jacqueline said doubtfully. "For an unfortunate baby of my acquaintance. Not a grandchild, no. I don't *think* I'm about to acquire one in the near future. The real function of this mess is to keep my hands occupied so I won't smoke."

"I think you just dropped a stitch."

"The baby won't know the difference," Jacqueline said callously. "And if you keep up those smart remarks, I'll let you do it. How is your work progressing?"

"I'm through, more or less. The reports aren't due till the end of the week, but I'm wrung dry."

With an air of guilt, Jacqueline shoved the knitting back into the purse and took out a pack of cigarettes. "I gather the others aren't as far along as you are. I haven't seen them for the last few days."

"They've been working. But most of them were at Gino's, yesterday."

"The same as always?"

"The same . . . I promised myself I wasn't going to talk about it."

"It's supposed to be cathartic to talk it out. Whatever it is."

"Oh, you know what it is. It will be a long, long time," said Jean softly, "before I can close my eyes at night without seeing him the way he looked, just before—"

"Forget it. I mean it literally, even if it does sound cruel. The time will come when you won't think of it. And much sooner than you believe."

"But that bothers me too. Death is such a final thing, it ought to . . . well, affect the world more than it does. It doesn't seem right that a man can die and leave so small a mark behind. Even someone like Albert. He was a human being, after all, and now the gap just closes up, and it's as if no one was ever there."

The waiter returned, and Jacqueline ordered food. As soon as the waiter had left, she leaned forward.

"What's bothering you, Jean?"

"Just nerves, I guess. . . . Except—do you think the police really believe it was suicide?"

"Why not?"

"Well, yesterday Dana mentioned, oh so casually, that she had had a drink or two with Lieutenant di Cavallo." Jean made a grimace of disgust. "She calls him Giovanni."

Jacqueline lit another cigarette.

"My dear infant, there are reasons why a man might drink with Dana."

"Oh, sure. . . . I didn't know you smoked."

"I didn't." Jacqueline regarded her cigarette with hatred. "I quit six months ago."

"Have we driven you to smoking?"

"You aren't the most restful companions a middle-aged lady could have. Look what you've gotten me into since I arrived in Rome."

"You don't know the half of it. I think we're all cracking up."

"Why, what else has happened?"

"What hasn't?" Jean bit into her sandwich and looked at

it with pleased surprise. "Hey, this place does have a slight edge over Gino's. . . . Well, for one thing, Dr. Scoville is back in town. Ahead of schedule."

"I know."

"You do?" Jean looked at the other woman, who smiled demurely. "Aha."

"Aha yourself. I'm having dinner with him tonight, but only because his revolting offspring have told him to leave them alone till Friday. The way Andy treats that poor man—"

"Yes, but he adores Andy. I feel sorry for Ann."

"He loves her too. But Andy is a rarity. It isn't often that a man has a child—and a son, at that—who is a conspicuous success in his own field. And on his own merit; there is a certain amount of nepotism in the academic world, but it doesn't carry a person far by itself."

"Ann is talented too," Jean said. "It would be ironic, wouldn't it, if she turned out to be the real genius in that family?"

"She would never let it show. She's been overshadowed by those two peacocks for too long. You must admit that Dr. Scoville is a very attractive man."

"Too old for me."

"I'm glad you think so. Dana doesn't. She was practically chasing him up the wall the other night."

"Mee-ow," Jean said, grinning. "What a pleasure it is to meet another feline female. Dana chases everything male. Even . . ."

"Even who?"

"I do get mad at her," Jean burst out. "Poor José; I guess he knows how to handle it, but after all, he's made his choice, and it doesn't seem fair to make it harder for him."

"I doubt that Dana makes it harder," Jacqueline said drily. "She doesn't strike me as his type. Women who see men as a challenge to be overcome are usually pretty insecure."

"Sure, sure, I know all the patter. I guess Dana is upset. She won't be back next year. Mama and Papa have cut off the funds. She'll have to go to work."

"What a catastrophe."

"I'm crying."

They grinned nastily at each other, and then Jacqueline said, "What's Ted's problem?"

"I think that girl he's engaged to is giving him a hard time. When I asked him when she was coming, he said she couldn't make it this year."

"Oh, dear."

"It may not be so bad at that. I think Ted and Ann could have a thing going, if they'd let themselves."

"What a pair of gossips we are. . . . Would you like some dessert?"

"No, thanks. What shall we do now?"

"Not much we can do. Everything is closed for the afternoon."

"We can walk down the Veneto and look in the windows."

"Good idea."

They strolled down the street, stopping at one of the newspaper kiosks, where Jacqueline bought several paperback books. Jean viewed her choice of reading matter with amusement.

"Still reading murder mysteries? What low taste."

"That's one of the advantages of middle age. You don't

have to pretend you're cultured. But I'm willing to be cultivated, if you can think of any intellectual sites that are open at this hour."

"There's a church not far from here that I'd love to show you. It's my favorite baroque church."

"The Gesù?"

"You do read something besides murder mysteries. . . . No, it isn't one of the big famous churches. It's a small place, a little jewel box of a church, all rose and ivory and gold, like the inside of a seashell by Fabergé. San Andrea al Quirinale. It's . . . well, it's my place. The place where I go when I want to be reassured about the world."

"I suppose many people have at least one place like that."

"Look at that gorgeous sweater," Jean exclaimed, stopping in front of a window. "I'll bet it costs thirty thousand lire. . . . Yes, it's funny, but we all have our own places here in Rome. Even Dana has admitted that when she's depressed she goes and sits on a rock in the Forum. That's not very original, but then neither is Dana."

"What about Michael?"

Jean laughed sharply.

"Michael. Would you like to see his place? We're practically on top of it. And five will get you ten Michael is there right now."

Jacqueline murmured agreement, and Jean led the way down the street. Her scraped knees were killing her by this time. They had almost reached the scene of her recent near-demise when she stopped under the grateful shade of a tall tree, and gestured.

"There it is."

Jacqueline studied the stairs that led up to an undistinguished church facade.

"Michael in a church?"

"Just wait," Jean said. "Just wait."

Jacqueline had read her guidebook; before they reached their final destination Jean saw comprehension begin to dawn on her face. But no amount of reading could prepare a viewer for the actuality.

It was an unpretentious place, only half a dozen small chapels opening off of a long, drab-painted corridor. The decorations were the source of the attraction. They were composed of human bones.

The long bones of arms and legs were piled in neat stacks, and human skulls formed the altars. Walls and ceilings were festooned with swags and scallops of vertebrae; a series of hip bones made a particularly ornamental pattern. Only the humbler members of the group had served as decorative sources; the more distinguished had been allowed to remain intact. They were present—some hanging from hooks, some lying flat in niches, all garbed in the drab-brown Capuchin habit. Their bony faces wore the same expression of fleshless laughter.

"Argh," Jacqueline said, and then smiled weakly at the single living member of the order, who was standing guard in the corridor. "I've read about this place. I had decided that under no circumstances would I visit it."

"I'm sorry," Jean said. "It was a dirty trick, sneaking you in here. I loathe the place myself. I'll never forget the first time Michael brought me here. I had *not* read about it."

"You should read Mark Twain's description," Jacqueline said. She glanced into the next chapel, which contained more of the same, and glanced quickly away.

"*The Innocents Abroad* is still one of the greatest travel books ever written. . . . I'd love to meet the man who thought this up."

"You can meet someone with the same type of mind," Jean said grimly. She gestured. "Look. What did I tell you?"

Michael was propped against the wall by the farthest chapel. He looked completely plastic and incapable of standing alone; the curve of his shoulders, back, and legs made a perfect arc. He was barefoot, and the shirt and flapping trousers he wore were of the same muddy hue as his tanned skin. He seemed to be unaware of them, and of the tourists who passed him, giggling or squealing according to their moods. His brooding profile, framed by the locks of his long dark hair, was bleached out by the artificial light.

"He looks frighteningly appropriate, standing there," Jacqueline said after a moment.

"Christ contemplating the damned in hell," Jean said. "Don't think Michael doesn't cultivate the resemblance. With a beard, he'd look like one of the paintings of Jesus."

"In the earliest representations of Christ, he is shown as young and beardless," Jacqueline said.

"Where do you learn these things?"

"My mind is a hopeless jumble of useless information," Jacqueline admitted. "Shall we steal quietly away?"

"He's seen us."

Michael's head turned. No other part of his body moved, but a smile spread slowly over his face.

"*Ciao*," he said amiably. "What are you two doing here?"

"*Sssh*," Jean said. "This is a chapel, isn't it?"

"It's okay; they know me here. Hey, Jake. How do you like it? This last chapel is the best. The three small skeletons are children of the nephew of some Pope or other."

After one incredulous glance Jacqueline turned her back on the arrangement Michael had been admiring. "I hate it, if you really want to know. In fact, I'm leaving. If you two want to stay—"

"Not me," said Jean.

"I'll come with you, then," Michael said. "I guess I've been here long enough."

"How long have you been here?"

"Geez, I dunno. An hour, maybe."

They emerged into the sunlight and air of the street, and Jean took a deep breath. Michael shook himself, like a dog coming out of the water; even his expression had changed. He looked at Jean as if seeing her for the first time that day.

"What happened to you?"

"I fell."

"In the middle of the Piazza Barberini," Jacqueline added.

"Old accident-prone," Michael said. "That's the second time in two days you've fallen on your face, love. Maybe you need a keeper."

Jacqueline made an odd sound, halfway between a cough and a groan. Clearing her throat, she asked,

"The second time? What happened the first time?"

"She took a tumble down the stairs at her place. Some

fool kid left a toy on the step."

"Trust me to step on it," Jean said. "If the light bulb on the landing hadn't burned out, I'd have been all right."

"The light was burned out," Jacqueline repeated.

"It happens all the time."

Michael had lost interest in the subject.

"What about a cup of coffee? If you have any bread, that is," he added disarmingly. "I'm flat broke."

"How were you planning to get home?" Jean inquired.

"Hitchhike. Walk. Who knows?"

"But we're supposed to meet the others at four," Jean said in exasperation. "Or weren't you planning to go to Ostia with us?"

They sat down at a table; outdoor cafés run three to a block on the Via Veneto. Michael ordered an espresso. "Sure, I'm going," he said. "I can be back by . . . what time is it now? Two-thirty. Plenty of time."

"Oh, you're all going swimming," Jacqueline said.

"Yes. Want to come along?"

"You do not know to whom you speak," Jean said. "She has a pool in her apartment compound. She doesn't have to mingle with the hoi polloi on a public beach."

Jacqueline did not respond to this provocative comment, which was unlike her. Jean realized that she was looking peculiar too. Her cheeks were damp with perspiration, and her glasses had slipped clear down to the tip of her nose. Jean had come to regard the glasses as indicative; like the formal props of a *noh* play, they showed which of Jacqueline's multiple personalities was uppermost. When the glasses were seated firmly on the bridge of her nose, the efficient librarian was in command; when they perched farther down and Jacqueline peered hazily over them, she was confused, or pretending to be. Occasionally the glasses rode high on the top of Jacqueline's head, held in place by her thick hair. Then she was feeling giddy and eccentric. The absence of the glasses usually meant that Jacqueline was in a feminine mood and following Dorothy Parker's famous advice.

Meeting Jean's curious eyes, Jacqueline took a deep breath and pushed her glasses firmly back into place.

"You might as well use my pool, if you want to swim. Most of the neighbors are away for the summer. There won't be anyone else in the pool."

"Great," Michael said happily.

"And you a revolutionary," Jacqueline said.

"But that's what the revolution is all about," Michael explained. "Making the effete luxuries of the Establishment available to everybody."

Again Jacqueline was uncharacteristically silent. Watching her, Jean saw the spectacles sliding slowly down her patrician nose.

As the afternoon passed, Jean decided she had become too fanciful about Jacqueline's glasses. Her mood improved rapidly, and after they had collected the other Sinners, who were assembled at Andy's apartment, she became her usual cheerfully caustic self.

When Jacqueline remembered that she was supposed to have a dinner date, she called the hotel and insisted that Scoville join them. The archaeologist agreed at once; when Jean saw him in his swimming trunks she could understand why he didn't mind parading around in a crowd of younger males. He made Ted look like an adolescent and Michael like a hairy white ape. Andy was the only male in the group whose shoulders were as broad as his father's.

The water felt so heavenly that Jean soon forgot the sting of her scraped legs; floating serenely she watched the sky darken and the shapes of the pines turn to black silhouettes. She felt more relaxed than she had for days. The pool had a night-lighting system, and the water shone like liquid sapphire.

The others seemed to be enjoying themselves. Ted swam solemnly with his nose just above water like an anxious dog. Scoville, in hilarious spirits, strutted like a rooster under Dana's admiring eyes. Dana was doing more admiring than swimming; her bikini was obviously designed for a minimum of physical activity.

Jacqueline was not swimming. Jean assumed she was being nice to José, for whom mixed bathing was on the forbidden list. For some reason she couldn't pin down, she found Jacqueline's claim that she was a poor swimmer unconvincing. It couldn't be shyness that made Jacqueline refrain; the shorts and halter she wore displayed as much of Jacqueline as a regulation bathing suit would have done, and Jean knew by now that Jacqueline would have walked down the Via Veneto in the same costume, with perfect self-possession, if she had a good and sufficient reason for doing so.

Later in the evening Jean pulled herself out of the water to rest for a while, and sat down on the wet tiles near Jacqueline and José. Lazily studying the two familiar faces, she was struck by the fact that they were equally familiar. She had not known Jacqueline long; yet she felt she knew her well, although Jacqueline was not verbose about her personal history. She came from a small New England town, and was now employed at one of the big Eastern universities. Her children—boy and girl—were both of college age. The girl was in graduate school, working for a doctorate. Jacqueline's father, a retired contractor, lived in California with one of Jacqueline's brothers. A prosaic, unvarnished history, so far as it went—and to Jean it did not go far in explaining the enigma that was Jacqueline. But then, she wondered dreamily, how many people can be adequately accounted for by a factual biographical paragraph or two? Perhaps some of Jacqueline's personality traits had been produced by the omissions in her biography. The most conspicuous omission was the absence of any reference to a husband. Jean assumed such a person had existed, but whether Jacqueline's silence was the result of grief for a beloved spouse prematurely deceased, or of contempt for a resented spouse belatedly divorced, she couldn't even guess.

As she watched, there was a howl of laughter from the far end of the pool and Andy surfaced, holding aloft a small dripping scrap of cloth. Shouting threats, Dana struck out toward him. Andy vanished, still holding his trophy.

"I knew the top of that bathing suit was going to come off sooner or later," Jean said sourly.

"There goes *il professore dottore* Scoville," murmured José, as the lean brown body cut the water in a spectacular dive from the small island in the deep end of the pool.

Jacqueline laughed.

"You two are a pair of prudes," she said.

"But Jean is a prude by nature," José said, smiling. "I, as your English adage says, have only acquired prudery. And it was not easy, I can tell you."

"I am not a prude," Jean said, without heat. "I just— Look at that, will you! Like father, like son . . ."

"The father wins," said José. "Andy has only the lady's bathing suit. *Il professore* has the lady. . . . Ah, yes; and what has happened to the lights at that end of the pool, I wonder? It is very dark there. . . ."

"The *portiere,*" Jacqueline said resignedly. "Someone has bribed him, I suppose. It always happens when there's a party. Look at that old wretch ogling Dana."

Jean had already noticed the *portiere,* an elderly man with a gray moustache. Dana wasn't the only one he ogled. After he had switched on the lights, there was no reason for him to linger; but he did, his mouth hanging open appreciatively as he watched the girls.

Jacqueline started to say something, but Jean didn't wait to hear what it was. She plunged into the pool, sending a spray of water high into the air. She swam in steady strokes toward the island and clung to it, her arm hooked over the edge of the stone coping. Dana had recovered the top of her suit and was making a big production of getting it back on. Someone—Michael—was behind her, tying the strings . . . or not tying them, as the case might be. There was a lot of splashing and yelling, as Dana tried to preserve her modesty by staying underwater—or tried not to stay underwater. . . .

A head popped up, right under her nose, and Jean let out

a squeal. In her dark bathing cap and suit Ann was almost invisible, except for her face. How different people's faces look without hair framing and softening them, Jean thought.

"Having fun?" she asked.

"Wonderful. This is nice of Jacqueline."

"What does your father think of her?"

"Oh, Sam is quite captivated," Ann said coolly. "She's handling him very well; nothing fascinates him like indifference."

Jean had heard equally cynical appraisals from other offspring, but coming from demure Ann, this remark did surprise her.

"Hey!" Standing up in the water like a seal, Andy called them. "We're playing hide and seek. Get moving, you two. I'm 'it,' and I'm after Jean. . . ."

He disappeared under the water and Jean, who knew his talent for breath holding, got moving as requested. The game was a success; it gave scope for every variety of acrobatics, practical jokes, and ingenuity. Finally everyone had been "it" but Jean. Ted was the poorest swimmer of the group, and had gotten caught most often, but he didn't seem to mind. Since they had all made it safely back to base, represented by Jacqueline and José, the last time, Ted was "it" again.

Diving down, Jean struck out for the dark end of the pool. The shadowy area behind the island made a good hiding place. When she came up for air the pool looked uncanny; there wasn't a person, or part of one, in sight, only the rippling blue water. Then a head popped up— sleek, dark. It was Michael. He took a deep breath and disappeared again. Ted was the next to come to the surface. He was wheezing and blowing; Jacqueline leaned out and shouted something. Jean caught a few words—something about "too tired."

Ted shook his head and resubmerged. His feet flopped agitatedly for a few seconds before they disappeared. Jean decided she had better go under and keep an eye out for him; with the lights reflecting off the water she couldn't see what was going on under the surface.

She had no warning, except the smallest whisper of sound, and that might have had any number of causes—a lizard scuttling across the pine-needle-covered ground, or the drop of an acorn. Then the darkness solidified and fell in on her. She had a moment of intense pain, but it was soon over; she never felt the water closing in over her head, filling her mouth and lungs.

The room was almost dark when she awoke from a nap she had had no intention of taking. Sitting up too suddenly, she clutched her spinning head and tried to orient herself. Slowly memory returned. She was in Jacqueline's apartment, and apparently Jacqueline had slipped her a Mickey in—

"No," Jean said aloud.

The word came out as a croak. Jean collapsed back onto the pillow. Her throat hurt, but that pain was minor compared to the throbbing headache that clamped over her skull. What had happened? This wasn't the first time she had awakened in Jacqueline's apartment; it was not the day Albert . . . Or was it? Had all the rest been a vivid, lifelike dream?

A light went on. It was a small, dim light, but it made Jean's head pound. She closed her eyes with a wordless mutter of protest.

"I was beginning to think that fool doctor was wrong," said a familiar voice. "Apparently you don't have concussion. Your head must be as hard as a rock."

"It feels cracked," said Jean thickly. She opened her eyes cautiously. It wasn't as bad this time. Jacqueline's head and shoulders cast a shadow over her face. "What happened?"

Jacqueline sat down on the edge of the bed. She was wearing a thin blue negligée, sleeveless and long, belted in around her waist, and her hair was loose, flowing down her back. She looked rather lovely—except for her face. It was colorless and hard, with lines in it Jean had never noticed before. The green eyes were slitted, like a cat's, and dull, without the gleam of humor that normally brightened them.

"What happened?" Jean repeated.

Jacqueline lit a cigarette.

"Do you remember anything?"

"We were playing hide and seek; Ted was 'it.' I remember, yes—I was in the dark part, watching Ted, and then . . . that's all." She looked helplessly at Jacqueline. "I don't remember anything else. What hit me?"

Jacqueline blew out a neat smoke ring and contemplated it critically.

"Apparently a chunk of that stone coping came loose and landed square on your head."

"But how—"

"You weren't hanging on to it—trying to pull yourself

out of the pool?"

"I don't think so. I can't remember. I feel so awful. . . ."

"I imagine you do. José pumped a couple of gallons of water out of you."

"José?"

"Mmmm. I gather the rest of you kid him when he tells you what a good swimmer he is. I couldn't swear to that, but he's an expert at resuscitation. And fast. If he hadn't been . . ."

She sat half turned away, smoking with quick, nervous puffs. Jean stared at her, conscious of an odd sensation in her stomach which had nothing to do with the water she had swallowed.

"I almost died," she said in a small voice. "Didn't I?"

Jacqueline swung around to face her, and Jean saw that the hand holding the cigarette was shaking.

"Yes, and you had a lot of nerve almost doing it in my pool. I'm too old for that sort of thing. It takes too much out of me."

"I'm sorry," Jean said meekly.

Jacqueline made a wild gesture of disgust, and then they both laughed—not hilariously, but they laughed. Jacqueline stood up and said, in a calmer voice,

"I'd better reassure the death watch. They've worn a hole in the rug pacing, and they're getting on my nerves."

"Is everybody still here?"

"No, just Ted and José. The two," Jacqueline mused, "with the greatest degree of social conscience? Anyhow, they insisted on staying, and I was glad to have the moral support. Ann wanted to stay, but she was a shaking wreck, so Andy took her home. And somehow or other Dana convinced Sam Scoville that her hand needed holding, so they went off together."

"I might have known."

"Sam was very touched at her affectionate nature," Jacqueline said drily.

"And Michael?"

"He just . . . left. As soon as we were sure you were going to be all right."

She went out, leaving the door open. Jean heard the murmur of voices, and the sound of the elevator coming up. When it had descended again, with her friends, Jacqueline came back.

"Could you eat anything, or does the idea repel you?"

"I could drink something. My throat hurts."

"I'll see what I can find."

She went out, and Jean dragged her pillows together and sat up. She felt fairly good, except for the headache. Experimentally she wriggled one toe, and watched it move with a new interest. How beautiful it was to be able to wriggle a toe—to move all the muscles of her body and feel them respond—to sense her breath moving in and out, and the pumping of her heart.

The sound of the elevator distracted her from these pensive thoughts, and instinctively she stiffened. She made herself relax; it was ridiculous to be so nervous. There were other apartments in the building, after all.

But the elevator stopped at their floor and the door buzzer sounded. Jacqueline's footsteps approached the door. Instead of opening it, she called out, "Who is it?"

Jean didn't hear the reply, but evidently Jacqueline was satisfied; the door opened and a murmured colloquy followed. Footsteps tapped down the uncarpeted hall.

"Michael," Jean said.

He stood in the doorway staring at her vacantly.

"You *are* all right," he said. "You're not dead."

"I told you she was all right." Jacqueline glided up behind him and came into the room, carrying a glass. "Why don't you go home and go to bed? You can't squat in the shrubbery all night; the *portiere* may understand, but the other tenants won't."

"All right, I'll go home," Michael said meekly. "I just wanted to make sure she was all right."

"I think we've established that fact."

"Hey, Jean. What happened?"

"Why ask me? I seem to have missed all the fun."

"Something hit you on the head?"

"So they tell me."

"You really don't remember anything?"

"For God's sake!" Jean yelled, and then clutched her head. "Get out of here," she mumbled. "That's all I need, you hanging around asking stupid questions."

"She really doesn't remember a thing, Michael," Jacqueline said.

"Amnesia?"

Standing straight and slim by the bed, Jacqueline looked him up and down with dispassionate interest. He was a pathetic sight, unkept and haggard; apparently Jacqueline's description of his whereabouts had been literal, for he was covered with twigs and dried leaves and dust.

"No," Jacqueline said, after a moment. "This is not a case of temporary amnesia, Michael. Something came down out of the dark and knocked her cold. That's all that happened, and that's all she'll ever remember."

"Uh-huh," Michael said. "I get it. You both ought to go to bed, get some sleep," he added, looking at them disapprovingly.

"As soon as you get out of here," Jean began, her voice rising dangerously.

Jacqueline took Michael by the arm and led him out. The elevator door had barely closed before the phone rang. There was an extension in the bedroom. Jacqueline took the call there, with a muttered exclamation in good gutter Italian.

"*Pronto!*" she yelled into the mouthpiece, and then her frown smoothed out. "Oh, Andy. Yes, yes, she's fine. No. Really; she's awake now. Want to talk to her?"

She handed Jean the phone.

"Hello," Jean croaked. "Andy, I don't want to talk, my throat hurts."

"I know, honey, and I'm sorry to call at this ungodly hour; but Ann's staggering around here like Medea—or do I mean Medusa?—accusing herself of failing you in the breach and chickening out, and various other crimes. If I could tell her you'll live—"

"You can't get rid of me that easily."

"I didn't realize your head was so hard," Andy said. Then his voice changed. The next words were so soft she could barely hear them, but they made a shiver go down her back. "I'm going to kill that cretinous *portiere.*"

"It wasn't his fault."

"He's supposed to keep the place in repair. It was criminal negligence, to say the least."

"Was that really what it was, a piece of the coping? I

didn't see a thing."

"Michael found the chunk on the bottom of the pool."

"Oh. Well, all's well that ends well," Jean said inanely.

"Right. I won't talk anymore. Good night, darling."

He hung up, leaving Jean staring at the telephone.

"Darling?" she repeated.

"Your near-demise has brought out all sorts of tender feelings," Jacqueline said. She took the telephone and put it back on the stand, but she kept her hand on it. "I wonder how long . . ." As Jean stared, she began to count. "Forty-one, forty-two . . . Not bad."

The phone rang.

"Hello," Jacqueline said. "Oh, yes, Sam, is it really you? It was good of Andy to call you; naturally you were concerned. Oh? Oh, she is . . . Of course she's upset. I do think it's terribly sweet of you to be so kind to her. . . . Well, you just tell the poor little thing that Jean is fine, and that I am going to blow Giorgio up, personally, tomorrow morning. . . . Yes, evidently that was what did the damage. Jean didn't see a thing, just felt the blow. . . . All right, Sam. Yes, you too."

She hung up and turned to face Jean, who was having trouble stifling her rising laughter.

"Talk about women being catty," she chuckled. "Dana wouldn't care if I were dead and buried. The professor just wanted you to know they had spent the night together."

"You think so?"

Jacqueline wasn't laughing. Absently she reached for another cigarette, lit it, and blew out a cloud of smoke. It wreathed her face like fog; and from the fog Jacqueline's voice said,

"That was the last. All of your friends have been heard from. Now which of them was it, do you think, who tried to kill you tonight?"

SIX

UNEMOTIONALLY Jean considered the question. It should have aroused a cry of disbelief or denial, or, at the least, of horror. Instead it seemed to crystallize a fact she had known, without admitting it, for a long time.

"I don't know," she said.

Abruptly Jacqueline sat down.

"Well, thank God for that."

"For what? That I don't know?"

"No, no. For accepting the idea. I was afraid you would think me hysterical. I keep forgetting how intelligent you are, under that Alice in Wonderland exterior. You look so blasted young. . . ."

"And I thought I was the one who was imagining things. Jacqueline, I'm not that clumsy, really I'm not. One accident, even two . . . But three in a row . . ."

"You honestly don't remember anything about tonight?" Jacqueline lit another cigarette. The incessant chain-smoking was the only sign of nerves she displayed; her hands were steady and her face showed only alert concentration. "I backed up your claim of ignorance as a matter of policy; obviously you didn't want anyone to get the idea that you suspect the identity of your attacker. But do you?"

"No, honestly. It could have been anybody. It was a madhouse; I don't suppose anyone kept track of anyone else. . . . Oh! You said José—"

Jacqueline shook her head reluctantly.

"Even José. He had left, to go up to the apartment for a minute. I didn't notice him after that, till he grabbed you away from me and tossed you down and started pushing your ribs around."

"Away from. . . . Now it all comes out. Were you the one who dragged me out of the pool?"

"Why do you think I was sitting on the sidelines like a dainty old chaperone?" Jacqueline snapped. "I was watching you; and a heck of a job it was, too, the way everyone was milling around. But in my hastily formed opinion you were safer in a small pool than you would have been in the ocean at Ostia."

"That is a point," Jean said slowly. "Jacqueline, you aren't a dainty old anything, you're a witch. How long have you had this suspicion?"

"Since Michael mentioned your first 'accident,' right after I had seen the scars of the second. I wasn't sure, of course; how could I be? But I started to get a nasty cold feeling in the pit of my stomach, and when you mentioned going swimming, it occurred to me what a perfect setup that would be for another accident. I couldn't warn you, I was afraid you would think I had flipped. All I could do was transfer your activities to a place where I thought I could keep an eye on you. When I think how nearly I failed, even then . . ."

"You saved my life," Jean said snuffily.

"Yes, well, let's both sit and cry about it, shall we? Anyhow," Jacqueline said grimly, "you'd better save your thanks. You aren't in the clear yet. And you won't be until we figure out who is doing this, and why."

"The 'why' is pretty obvious, isn't it?"

"Yes, in a way. In another way—no, curse it! You're thinking of Albert's death. So am I; it more or less rises up and hits you in the face. But don't you see that that assumption only raises another, stickier problem? You were the one to find Albert. Not only was he capable of communication when you found him, but he actually did communicate. That's such a classic situation it's almost corny. But in every thriller I've ever read, the witness is only in danger while he remains silent. The murderer has to shut him up before he can spill the essential clue. But you have already spilled it! Just to keep the record straight—Albert did not say anything, or write anything other than what you have already described to me—and to all your friends, and the entire police department?"

"No."

"And there was no object in that room which might have provided a clue to a hypothetical murderer? No item—no discrepancy, or inconsistency—that the police could have missed, but that might have significance to someone else?"

"No." Jean shook her head. It still hurt, but she was far too preoccupied to notice a minor thing like physical pain. The relief of being able to talk about the subject that had harassed her subconscious was enormous. She also had a lively interest in the topic; it involved no less a matter than her life or death. "Don't you think I've been over it and over it in my mind? I can still see that room vividly when I close my eyes; it was absolutely bare, except for—him. He said nothing, he wrote nothing, except what I've already described—as you say, to half the city of Rome. They didn't even believe me," she added glumly.

"Another good point. In attempting to silence you, the murderer runs the risk of drawing attention to the very thing he wants to hide. He's obviously a capable person; Albert's death was neatly planned. Why would he take such a risk unless you present a very real and immediate danger to him?"

"You keep saying 'him.' "

"The standard male chauvinist pronoun of indefinite reference," Jacqueline said, with a smile that was not very convincing.

"I'd love it to be Dana," Jean said wistfully.

Jacqueline burst out laughing.

"Well, thank goodness you've got some gumption," she said approvingly. "If you collapsed into a quivering jelly of terror it would present a problem."

"I'm really scared," Jean said in a low voice. "I realized tonight how much—how much I want to go on being alive."

"Then it's up to us to keep you that way," Jacqueline said briskly. "And we're really starting from scratch, Jean. It must be one of the six. But I have no idea which one; not even a suspicion."

"You're sure it's one of them?"

"Well, let's be logical. Conceivably Albert might have been killed by an outsider—some private grudge. The exits at the church weren't closed until sometime after the attack took place and the killer could have escaped into the anonymity of the street before the alarm was sounded. He would have no reason to linger—unless he was one of the Seven Sinners, who were following a schedule. On that basis I eliminate the other tourists who were caught in the net that day. The lieutenant isn't as casual as he sounds. He will have checked them all."

"That's reasonable. But the killer didn't plan on my finding Albert. He might have lain there for hours before anyone found him. We'd have all cleared out by then."

"True, but irrelevant. Albert would have been identified eventually; his connection with all of you would have been traced, and the police would have discovered that you were there, on the spot, at the time of his death. The murderer's plan was to make his death look like suicide, and it succeeded admirably."

"Right."

"None of this knocks out the possibility of an outsider having committed the crime. But the attempts on you are something else again. I'll grant that an unknown party could be following you around, shoving you under cars, and turning out lights in strategic places. But tonight there was no one in the pool except your friends."

"And Dr. Scoville."

"And," Jacqueline repeated, "Dr. Scoville. . . . Oh, no, that really is farfetched."

"Still, so far as opportunity is concerned, we have to include him. It wouldn't be hard to set up an alibi. . . . Look here, Jake, he said something about taking a train the next day, but how do we know he did? Suppose he took a plane instead, later in the day? It would be almost impossible to prove, one way or the other; he wouldn't need his passport for travel within Italy."

"What about motive?"

"Oh, motive be damned. We haven't even started on that yet."

"Okay, let's include him," Jacqueline said callously. "That brings our suspect list back to the original seven. I'm assuming you wouldn't half drown yourself just to add verisimilitude to an otherwise unconvincing narrative."

"Bald and unconvincing narrative."

"I'm glad to see your generation reads something besides Leonard Cohen and *Steppenwolf*. . . . Have we now limited our suspects to seven?"

"I know it's unlikely that an outsider could have sneaked in," Jean said stubbornly. "But that pool area was dark. It isn't impossible, Jake."

"You are missing the point," said Jacqueline, reaching for another cigarette. "An outsider might pursue you. But how does he know he should? No one except your friends—and the police—know that Albert was alive when you found him."

Jean was silent. Jacqueline went on, in a more kindly tone,

"I know you don't want to admit it. You're fond of all your friends—even Dana, in a fashion. But the facts are inescapable."

"I know. And I appreciate your effort to make this seem like an intellectual game. But it isn't a game."

"It's a dangerous game. As soon as it's morning I'm going to call our friend the lieutenant."

"You can't do that."

"Why not, for heaven's sake?"

"They won't believe you. The lieutenant has already decided Albert's death was suicide, and that suits him fine. He isn't going to reopen the case on the basis of what has happened to me. We may be sure that these accidents weren't accidents, but he'll just laugh. Anyhow, what could he do about it?"

"The police could check alibis," Jacqueline said stubbornly. "There have been three separate attacks on you; surely they could weed out some of our suspects by finding out where they were at the time—"

"At what time? You were on the spot tonight; can you eliminate anyone? The stair incident is the vaguest of all; it might even have been coincidence. We don't know when the light was turned off, and when the toy was left on the stair. The car incident—we already know that Michael was in the neighborhood at the right time. Dana and Ted were both downtown that day; she planned to do some shopping, and Ted was having lunch with a man who lives near the Spanish Steps. That's only a couple of blocks from the Piazza Barberini. I'll bet the others will be just as hard to pin down."

"It's interesting," Jacqueline said. "My generation automatically turns to the police when anything goes wrong; yours has an instinctive mistrust. Still, you have a point."

"They can't do anything we can't do," Jean argued. She pulled herself up in bed, fired with new energy. "Jake, this must go back to Albert's death. If we could prove that wasn't suicide—"

"How?"

"Let's think! There must be something."

Jacqueline settled herself more comfortably.

"There is nothing in the physical circumstances of his death," she said thoughtfully. "The weapon was found nearby, where it could have fallen from his hand. The nature of the wound was such that it could have been self-inflicted. Di Cavallo asked whether he was right- or left-handed, and nodded in that smug way of his; so clearly that part of it made sense."

"He was right-handed," Jean said. "Which means that he could have been killed by a right-handed person standing behind him. If you were planning to cut someone's throat, that's where you would stand. To avoid being covered with blood."

Jacqueline gave a look of mingled admiration and surprise.

"You're a cold-blooded little creature, aren't you?"

"I can be girlish and squeamish when I want to be," Jean said grimly. "But, as we agreed, this isn't a game. . . . Obviously the murderer stood behind him. You don't advance on a victim waving a knife; you come up behind his back. You gain the element of surprise, you avoid incriminating bloodstains, and you produce the kind of wound that looks like suicide. If I can think of these things, a clever murderer surely would."

"There would have to be some blood. On the killer's hands and arms."

"It was a hot day, everyone wore short sleeves, or none. And there is a stream of running water in that room. The overflow from the conduit in the wall."

"Good Lord," Jacqueline muttered. "I'd forgotten that.

. . . I thought perhaps the murderer had chosen that room because of its remote location, but maybe there was another reason. What about fingerprints?"

"I don't think much of the fuzz, but I'm sure they would have looked for fingerprints."

"And found only Albert's. But the murderer couldn't have worn gloves without being rather conspicuous."

"He could have stuffed them in his pocket and gotten rid of them later. Nobody searched us."

"We don't seem to be making much progress," Jacqueline said. "What about alibis for Albert's death?"

"Hopeless. We were all more or less lost. Besides, do they know when the attack took place? Albert didn't die until later."

"Yet that avenue needs exploring. I can ask, in a casually nosy fashion. It seems to me that Ann and Ted were together much of the time."

"Yes, but alibis like that aren't any good. Michael and Dana were together part of the time too; but they might lie for each other. Actually, both of them were on the lowest level only minutes before I found Albert."

"I," said Jacqueline, "have sort of an alibi. Don't look so surprised; if you haven't suspected me, you're pretty dim. I got tired of your bloody ruins and went up to look at those lovely frescoes in the chapel of St. Catherine. The priest selling tickets must have seen me go up, and anyone going down would have to pass him. When I went back down to look for you, Ann and Ted were talking to the priest on duty. If they had been there for any length of time . . ."

Jean shook her head.

"We're on the wrong track. The police could do this sort of thing much more effectively than we can, and I'm sure we can't narrow it down to a single suspect. It's motive we ought to explore. Why would anybody want to kill Albert? That is the one aspect of the case we can investigate better than the police. We know the people involved."

"It's also the weakest part of the case. If you know anything about murders, real or fictional, you know that people have killed for reasons which would strike you and me as ludicrously inadequate. That's why motive is, quite rightly, a secondary consideration in police investigations."

They stared at one another in despairing silence. Then Jacqueline got up and went to the French doors onto the balcony. She threw back the heavy wooden shutters. The sun had just lifted above the horizon. A pearly hush lay upon the drowsy world, and through the still cool air a burst of bird song rippled.

For several seconds Jacqueline stayed at the window, her arms raised. With an art critic's eye for line and color, Jean commended the pose. The pale sunlight on Jacqueline's unbound hair was like a wash of gold.

Then the poised statue turned and said in a flat, weary voice,

"We're both shot. Maybe we can think better after we get some sleep. There are twin beds in this room; do you mind if I—"

"Why should I mind?"

"I hope you don't. Because, whether you mind or not, from now on I'm sticking to you like the proverbial limpet. You are moving into this apartment, and you are not going out of it without me."

"We may be all wrong," Jean said. "About everything."

"Maybe. But I'm not taking any chances. Tomorrow we'll start detecting."

"If we only knew what to detect!"

"Don't worry about that," Jacqueline said coolly. "I'll think of something."

"Seven saints?" José said. "Where did you get that notion? Oh . . ." There was the slightest possible check in his voice. "From Albert, of course."

They were standing in front of the altar of Santa Cecilia, looking at Maderno's famous statue of the saint. In the past forty-eight hours Jacqueline had carried on a mad rush of sightseeing, dragging with her every available member of the Seven. Only four of them were with her that day; Dana had flatly refused to come, and Andy was barricaded in his room with coffee pots and ice bags, and Ann in devoted attendance. The résumés were due in two more days.

Jean knew why Jacqueline was doing this; at least she knew what the motive was, even if she couldn't understand the underlying logic. Santa Cecilia was an old church, and it contained some lovely things, but it was not one of the major attractions in the city.

"I guess it does sound silly," Jacqueline admitted ingenuously. "But you know, I got to counting, and I did find seven of them."

"Santa Cecilia being one?" Ted regarded the statue with interest. "Do you know that after they cut her head off, she lay for three days on the floor of her bath, fully sensible, and joyfully awaiting her crown of martyrdom?"

Jean snickered, and José smiled even as he shook his head.

"Ted, you do not play fair. You quote from a popular account of the saint's life. Books written for children always sound foolish when they are quoted to intelligent adults."

"Anyhow, you're misquoting," Jacqueline said severely. Taking a small book from her purse, she brandished it. "This is the Penguin *Dictionary of Saints*, and the writer is quite skeptical of such legends."

"May I?" José held out his hand, and Jacqueline gave him the book. He leafed through it. "Yes, here we are. 'Sentenced to be stifled to death in the bathroom of her own house, the heat and steam failed to suffocate her, so a soldier was sent to behead her. He struck three ineffective blows, and she was left to linger three days before she died.' Improbable, but not as ridiculous as your version, Ted."

Jean glanced at Michael, who stood a little to one side. He was staring steadily at the statue, which lay in a glass-fronted case under the altar.

"Oh, I don't mind these stories," Ted said tolerantly. "They are pretty stories—if you discount the basic Freudian hangup about virginity. . . ." He dodged the fist José raised, and went on, "The part I like best is the description of finding the saint's body."

"That isn't in my book," Jacqueline said.

"Good, then I can tell you. In 1599, the tomb of the saint, in the catacomb, was opened. I do not know why.

They were a morbid lot, your ancestors. . . . A great party of dignitaries was present, including the artist Stefano Maderno. And behold, there lay the body of the saint, uncorrupted, unchanged; her garments still modestly arranged, as you see them in the statue, her averted face veiled. The body was brought here and reintombed; and Maderno ran home and made his statue—a literal copy, according to his own account, of the actual body of the saint as she looked fifteen centuries after her death."

They all turned to contemplate the life-sized marble. The figure was that of a young woman lying on her side, with her knees bent and her limp hands gracefully disposed. The features were indistinct, but around the neck the line made by the executioner's sword was clearly visible.

"Pathetic," Michael said, breaking his own prolonged silence. "Bathetic. Schmaltz. Kitsch. Let's go, it's cold in here."

The others followed him. Blinking in the sunlight of the portico, Ted turned to Jacqueline.

"What are you doing now, collecting virgin saints? We have seen—yes, six churches." He turned his wide, innocent stare on Jacqueline. "What is the seventh?"

"Santa Prisca," said Jacqueline coolly.

Michael let out a howl.

"Good God, that's clear out on the Aventine. You don't want to see that one, Jake. It's a drag. And it's probably closed. And besides—"

"It's a beautiful day," Jacqueline said, settling her glasses firmly on the bridge of her nose. "And the Aventine is beautiful on a beautiful day. And besides—"

"Well?"

"If you're broke again, which I suspect you are, you'll have to stick with me or you won't get any lunch."

"Thanks be to God, I have no such problem," said Ted piously. "I will see you all tomorrow, at Gino's?"

"Maybe not," Jacqueline said. "I'm going sightseeing again."

"Not more churches?" Michael said pathetically.

"Oh, yes. Tomorrow we start on the seven pilgrimage churches. There were," Jacqueline said sweetly, "seven, weren't there?"

"You're flipping," Andy said. "Or else you're going in for numerology. Why the passionate interest in septets?"

He looked, that evening, as close to collapse as a robust, tanned young specimen can look. There were circles, not only under his eyes, but all around them.

"Stop talking and eat," his father ordered.

Obediently Andy shoved a huge forkful of spaghetti into his mouth. The others watched as he tucked in the dangling ends, *all' italiano.* As soon as Andy became vocal again, he said mildly,

"Not that I'm not proud of my skill in eating spaghetti, but do you all have to stare at me? I have eaten before, I am eating now, and I will eat again. It's no big deal."

"You may have eaten, but not recently," Ann said, looking at him anxiously. "We ought to thank Jacqueline for insisting on taking us out to supper. You can't go on working without food or sleep. I'm going to slip a couple of those sleeping pills in your coffee tonight."

"I do thank Jacqueline," said Scoville, with a smile at

that lady, who dimpled and batted her eyelashes. She was not wearing her glasses. "But you should have called me earlier, Ginger. I'd rather have this young idiot lose every fellowship under the sun than get sick."

"Like hell you would," said Andy, through another mouthful. "Better dead than dishonored, that's the motto in this family. . . . Okay, that takes care of the appetizer. While we wait for the next course, may I change the subject to something more interesting than my personal habits? I repeat: why the passionate interest in sevens, Jake?"

Fumbling in her purse in search of cigarettes, Jacqueline didn't answer at first. They were eating at a trattoria in Trastevere, one of the few that had escaped the tourism craze. Twilight had fallen, the soft blue dusk of a Roman summer; and they sat outside, with a thick hedge separating them from the bustle of the pedestrian traffic, and an awning protecting them overhead. Between the pots in which the bushes of the hedge were planted, a lean, suspicious cat wove in and out, casing the diners for potential handouts.

"Mystic number," Jacqueline said finally. Triumphantly she produced a battered pack of cigarettes; Scoville flung himself across the table to light one for her, and she went on, "It keeps cropping up, doesn't it? Saints, churches, hills—"

"And sinners," Andy interrupted. "Don't beat around the bush. You're trying to figure out Albert's last words, aren't you? There's another seven for you, by the way—the Seven Last Words of Christ."

He looked at Jean. Everyone else looked at Jean—the

three Scovilles, Jacqueline and Michael. Michael hadn't been invited, but he was there anyway. It was hard to get rid of Michael. He was too big to evict physically, and too obtuse to notice hints. If his ubiquity had increased, his loquacity had not. Tonight he sat in silence, his eyes moving from one speaker to the next; he had slid down as far as the straight chair would permit him to do, with his legs stretched out. He was feeding long strings of spaghetti to the cat, a lean black-and-white tom, which absorbed the pasta like a true Roman.

"I thought you didn't believe me," Jean said.

"Of course we do," Ann said, a little too quickly.

"So maybe I imagined it," Jean said defiantly. "No one else saw anything. There wasn't a sign of any mark left when the police got there."

"A lot of heavy flat feet scuffled through the room," Andy said. "According to you, the marks were indistinct to begin with."

Jean looked at him gratefully. "You believe me."

"We all believe you," Ann said. "But perhaps you misinterpreted what you saw. The last reflex contraction of muscles—"

"All right, Ginger," Scoville said. "What difference does it make? If the gesture had meaning, it is lost forever now. The vagaries of a dying man—"

The waiter brought the next course, and for a few moments they were all quiet, sampling the entrees. Then Andy said,

"Maybe so. But it's bound to haunt you, isn't it? What did he want to say all that badly? Why can't we see it?"

"It's been driving me crazy," Jacqueline admitted. "I

have that type of inconsequential mind. . . . But I'll be darned if I can think of anything."

"You can't? I can think of only too many things. This city is swamped with sevens. Albert's saints, the pilgrimage churches, and the hills. . . . There's a good quiz question for you. Name the seven hills."

The others looked blank, but Jacqueline appeared to be enjoying the game. She began counting on her fingers.

Scoville cleared his throat.

"I fail to see—"

"There are lots more," Andy grinned. "How about the Seven Churches of Asia? Ephesus, Smyrna, Pergamus—"

Michael assumed an upright position with such abruptness that the cat, who had learned to suspect any violent movements, vanished behind a shrub.

"Of all the crap . . . You might as well try to find some application in Beethoven's *Seventh Symphony.* Or in seven-card stud."

"Seven Wonders of the World," Jacqueline contributed. "None of them in Rome, though . . ."

"Seven Sages," Jean said wildly. "The Seven Sleepers of Ephesus. Seven Against Thebes. The Seven Deadly—"

She stopped speaking abruptly, and Andy, who had been watching her, said mildly,

"Your acquaintance with sin is purely nominal, my lamb. But it makes a suggestive list, doesn't it? Seven sins and seven sinners. They're such unusual sins, not at all the kind of thing you might expect. My favorite is Languid Indifference—the original Greek *acidia* sounds better. . . . Anger is Michael, of course, and Pride—spiritual pride— must be José's sin. Gluttony doesn't seem appropriate to any one of us, offhand."

"Me," Jean said. She could not have said why, but she didn't like the turn the conversation had taken. "I adore food. I'd be a little fat girl if Vanity weren't stronger than Gluttony."

"Sorry, but Vanity is not one of the Seven," Andy said. "Vainglory, yes; but it isn't the same thing. Now Unchastity—"

"Stop it," Ann said. "It isn't nice to talk about someone who isn't here to defend herself."

There was a general explosion of laughter, and Andy said fondly,

"Very good. That's one of the few catty remarks I've ever heard you make. Now, as the antithesis of the Seven Sins there are also Seven Virtues—"

"I think we've had enough sevens," Scoville interrupted. "Not only are your ideas getting farfetched, but you are ignoring one vital fact."

"What's that?" Jacqueline asked meekly.

"None of your categories is ordered. The number seven can only refer to one member of a septet. How do you know which, if the lists aren't numbered?"

"Good gracious," Jacqueline murmured. "I declare, that is true, isn't it? How clever you are, Sam."

Scoville expanded visibly; and Jean, after one look at Jacqueline's studiously sweet expression, bent over and pretended she was calling the cat.

"Dana can't make it," Michael reported. "She says she has to get some work done."

"You sound as if you don't believe her," Jean said.

"I think she's working on dear old Dad Scoville. And vice versa."

"I thought he had better taste."

Michael kicked a stone. It rattled along the sidewalk and smacked into a tree.

"Your girl friend turned him down. He's on the rebound—or trying to show her he doesn't give a damn."

"Oh," Jean said disinterestedly. She turned her back on the splendid tree-lined boulevard and stared out across the space beyond. It was sunk below the modern street level, and its expanse was filled with a clutter that would have struck a modern city planner as extremely unsightly. Fragments of brick walls, covered with ivy and half veiled by weeds, rose up in unconnected sections. Columns of all sizes and shapes and conditions stood randomly about: columns of white marble and dark-red granite, half columns and lonely column bases, columns in rows and circles and colonnades. The Roman Forum, enclosed on the far side by the tree-darkened slope of the Palatine, was almost as crowded that day as it had been in its glory, when merchants and senators and slaves thronged its shops.

"Who are we waiting for?" Michael asked.

"Nobody asked you to wait. In fact, nobody asked you to come in the first place."

"Dana told me to tell you—"

"And how did you happen to know Dana was meeting us here?"

Jean turned, leaning against the iron fence that kept impetuous and impecunious tourists from leaping down among the ruins. "I keep thinking somebody's following me, Michael. It can't be paranoia; it must be you."

"You never used to object to my following you."

"You didn't—oh, forget it. Why don't you go away? You've seen the Forum a dozen times, and you don't care anything about the seven Caesars."

"What do you mean, seven? Who says there were seven?"

Jean gave him a long, appraising look. Considering the subject, it was inevitable that the pertinent quotation should come to her mind. The lean and hungry look was quite pronounced these days. Even Michael's eyes looked strained; they were constantly moving, darting quick glances from side to side. She had never noticed the habit before. The word "hunted" came into her mind.

"You think too much," she said flippantly. "Such men are dangerous."

"I've been thinking about sevens. We all have; we're hung up on numbers. What is that woman up to, Jean?"

"What do you mean?"

"Two weeks ago you'd never heard of her. Now she's practically adopted you. What does she want? Are you sure she isn't queer?"

Jean didn't know whether to laugh or be angry. Anger won; her nerves weren't at their best. And in her anger she broke the rule she and Jacqueline had been observing from the first—never to express their suspicions openly.

"Yes, she's queer! It's queer, these days, to put yourself out for another human being. Just because she's trying to keep me from getting killed—"

Michael's eyes shifted, and Jean turned. Jacqueline had arrived. She was wearing sunglasses: with the inquisitive green eyes hidden, she looked remote and unfamiliar. Her short, sleeveless dress was golden yellow. The purse was held tightly in the curve of her arm.

"Sorry I'm late," she began. "I couldn't get—what's wrong with you two?"

"So that's it," Michael said softly. "They weren't accidents. You believe that too."

"I didn't mean to say that," Jean babbled. "I wasn't thinking. I mean—"

"Wait a minute." Jacqueline put a hand on her arm. "Did you say 'too,' Michael?"

"What do you think I've been following her around for?" Michael made a violent gesture. "I don't stick around where I'm not wanted unless I've got a reason. Why do you think I've been prowling around your apartment half the night?"

"You've been what?"

"Be quiet, Jean," Jacqueline interrupted. "I knew he was there. Giorgio told me."

"Why, that fat pirate!" Michael exploded. "After all the glasses of *bianco* I've bought him, and the sad stories I told him about unrequited love and a rival—"

"He thinks you are a very *simpatico* young romantic," Jacqueline said. "But I paid him. Grow up, Michael. . . . Are you trying to tell us that you've been watching Jean in order to protect her? That you are also suspicious of her so-called accidents?"

"Right on."

"Why?"

"Why was I suspicious? Why were you?"

"All right," Jacqueline said, with a sigh. "What else

strikes you about the situation?"

"That it's tied in with Albert's death," Michael said promptly. "Hell, it's obvious, isn't it? You think it was murder, not suicide."

"What do you think?"

"No reason why not. If I ever met a cat who was asking to be murdered, it was Albert."

Jean was still speechless. Jacqueline said calmly,

"That's an interesting contribution. Our problem has been that we couldn't figure out why anybody would want to kill him."

"Good Lord, there are fifty reasons."

"Such as?"

"Ah, hell," Michael said. "You're probably being too logical. There never is a good reason for murder, is there? According to your ethos, anyhow. Except maybe to save a crippled child from an ax murderer, and like that. But murders are committed every second of the day, for all kinds of lousy reasons. Albert was a born victim. He was nosy, rude, and insensitive; sooner or later he was bound to stick his nose into something that was none of his business."

"You're suggesting that he was killed because he had stumbled on someone's secret? You know who the suspects are, don't you?"

Michael's eyes flickered.

"Sure. That's obvious. The Seven—your mystic number."

"Which implies," said Jacqueline patiently, "that one of you nice young intelligent kids has a guilty secret. It's hard to believe, Michael."

"Nice young intelligent kids," Michael repeated, with a note of wry amusement. "Lady, you are really out of it. We are all cruddy with guilty secrets."

He looked from one of them to the other, and suddenly anger seized him.

"You think I'm kidding? All right, I'll show you. What time is it? If we hurry, maybe we can catch him."

"Who? What are you talking about?"

Michael was already moving, pulling Jean by the hand. She held back, but he was too strong for her. Jacqueline followed, demanding explanations. Michael paid no attention to either.

"Taxi," he said. "There may be time if we take a taxi."

He caught one by the simple expedient of stepping out in front of it, and shoved the women in.

"Piazza Colonna," he told the driver. "*Subito, pronto, fast*—okay?"

The traffic was heavy, and the drive took longer than Michael liked; he kept up a stream of muttered complaints, and absolutely refused to answer questions. When they reached the piazza, marked by the tall circular column of Marcus Aurelius, he pushed them out of the taxi as ruthlessly as he had pushed them in. Jacqueline tossed the driver some money; she didn't get to collect her change.

Michael dragged them into the famous pastry-shop café that occupied one corner of the piazza. As usual, it was crowded with people.

"They're still there," Michael said. "I can see them. Move up to the door, but don't go out. Third table on the right, in the outside row."

Through the doorway Jean could see the expanse of the Galleria, a favorite meeting place for opulent tourists. It was a long glass-covered shopping arcade, and the café had tables occupying a considerable stretch of the paving. It was one of the more expensive cafés in the city; a musical ensemble played, and the prices, like the pastry, were rich.

"I don't even know who I'm looking for," Jean said irritably. "What—"

Then she saw the pair Michael indicated.

Ted was sitting with his back to them, but by that time Jean knew her friends well enough to recognize them from any angle. The girl across the table from him was facing the doorway. Jean could see her features plainly. It was someone she had never seen before.

She wasn't a pretty girl. Her features were too sharp and too strongly marked for beauty. But it was a striking face, the sort of face some people might turn to stare at. The girl was as dark-skinned as a Sicilian, but the high cheekbones and fierce, slightly hooked nose had never come out of an Italian village. Her black hair, swept back from a high forehead, was held in place by a band of brightly embroidered fabric, but that was her only concession to feminine vanity. She wore no jewelry and no makeup; the open-necked tan shirt showed a slim throat whose tendons stood out with the vigor of her conversation. She was angry or distressed, or both; the black eyes flashed and the wide mouth shaped vehement words.

"She came after all," Jean said, bewildered. "Ted's girl friend. Why don't we go and—"

Michael's hand clamped tightly over her shoulder.

"No, you idiot! That isn't Ted's fiancée."

"How do you know?"

"He showed us her picture."

"Yes, but—"

"But you don't remember it. Faces are my thing," said Michael. "That girl is not Ted's girl. My God, how could you forget a face like that?"

"She looks like a young hawk," Jacqueline said softly. "A beautiful, predatory falcon."

"Oh, she's beautiful," Michael said, as if it didn't matter. "And Ted has been meeting her here every day at about this time. This place is 'way out of our usual beat. I guess that's why he thought it was safe. I happened to come through this way last week, and spotted them then."

"Once? How did you know they would be here today?"

"They were here yesterday and the day before," Michael said. "I checked."

"Why?"

The dark girl looked up, and Michael pulled Jean back out of the doorway. She smacked at his hand.

"Stop pushing me around. I don't understand all this, Michael. Why the secrecy?"

"I didn't initiate the secrecy," Michael pointed out. "Ted did. We know each other's friends; why hasn't he introduced her to any of us? Why do they meet here, in this tourist trap, unless it's to avoid attention?"

"But it's Ted's business whom he meets," Jean exclaimed. "If he has a thing going with some girl, and a fiancée back home—"

"Look at them," Jacqueline interrupted. "Does that look like romance to you?"

The two had risen. Ted still had his back to them, but even his back radiated anger. He stood stiff as a judge, his slender body drawn up to its full height and his hands clenched into fists. The girl, leaning slightly forward, continued to speak; she looked as if she were spitting the words out. Her body was as slim as a boy's and the tanned forearms, braced on the table, were corded with muscle.

Suddenly she turned on her heel and marched away. The waiter came hurrying up, and Ted, who stood staring after her, relaxed. He started to turn. The three conspirators hastily withdrew. Scuttling like the eavesdroppers they were, led by Michael, they made their escape into the street and didn't stop moving until they had ducked into an alleyway a block down the Via del Corso.

"I still don't understand." Jean was the first to speak.

"God, you're dumb," Michael said disgustedly.

"Maybe we're the ones who are jumping to conclusions," Jacqueline said. "At least I'm pretty sure I jumped to the same one you are now perching uncomfortably upon. . . . Jean, what would you guess that girl's nationality to be?"

"Could be a lot of things."

"True. I said guess."

"Well—Israeli, I suppose. She could be Italian or Spanish, but the bone structure isn't right. Though I've seen a few Spaniards with cheekbones like that."

"The Moors were in Spain for a long time," said Jacqueline.

Michael gave her a meaningful look and nodded.

"Yeah. It's the same conclusion. . . . That face comes out of the Near East, Jean. She could be an Israeli, a sabra—

native-born. Or she could be an Arab."

"Like—Albert."

"Like Albert. And before you start babbling about coincidence, let me remind you who's at war with whom."

"I can't believe it."

"That the girl is an Arab? If she's Israeli, why doesn't Ted bring her around and introduce her? We're not a bunch of scandal-mongering old ladies; nobody is going to write anonymous letters to his girl."

Jean continued to shake her head.

"We must be wrong. Wrong about everything. A person could have three accidents in a row; wilder things have happened."

"We can't assume that," Jacqueline said. "We can't afford to take chances. But I don't like this new development you've tossed at us, Michael. If we're getting into the hairy underworld of espionage. . . ."

"Oh, no," Jean groaned. "That I won't believe!"

"It does open vistas," Jacqueline argued. "And it provides a possible motive for murder. That's all we're looking for at this stage—possibilities."

"Oh, you're looking for motives, are you." Michael's flat voice turned the question into a statement. "How many have you come up with?"

"Several," Jacqueline said calmly. She saw Jean's look of surprise, and said nastily, "Oh, come on, Jean, don't be so naïve. I told you—every human being is at least a dozen different people. How much do you really know about your friends? Albert was an inquisitive man. If he had stumbled on a secret that threatened someone's security—"

"Such as?"

"This is all theoretical. But take José. He loves his work and knows he's lucky to be allowed to do it; the Church considers other matters more important than a man's talent. If Albert had caught him in some pecadillo, it would threaten his work. The order would certainly discipline him, and without its support he couldn't go on with his studies."

"Go on," Jean said.

"Ann. I've seen her look sick when Albert made a pass at her. What may appear to be only fastidiousness might be a well-developed neurosis, and Albert was not the man to take a hint. If he cornered her down there, and got nasty about it . . ."

"My God," Michael said. "You ought to be locked up. Well?"

"Dana," said Jacqueline coolly. "I refer now to an incident everyone else seems to have forgotten—Albert's accusation that someone had robbed him. You all scoffed at this because of Albert's poverty; but that doesn't prove he might not have had some object of value with him. A family heirloom, perhaps. Dana's need of money is notorious."

"No more notorious than mine," Michael muttered.

"You have a source of income adequate for your needs. I'm inclined to accept your claim that you don't care about money. I could be wrong, though."

Michael looked dazed. He shook his head, muttering. Jean felt dazed too. Unwillingly, she remembered the look on Michael's face that day, when he had confessed his carefully hidden phobia. Could such a need be strong enough to drive a sufferer to murder? If Albert had found Michael in that closed-in room and, as a malicious joke, barred his way out . . .

"No," she said in a strangled voice. "It's weird. All of it."

"*She's* weird," said Michael, jerking a thumb toward Jacqueline. "What a mind . . . All right, now that I've given you a motive for Ted, what about Andy?"

"I'm still working on him," Jacqueline said. "And on you."

"All this is the wildest speculation," Jean insisted. "You haven't proved a thing."

"One thing," said Jacqueline. "The futility of this kind of theorizing. I was just trying to convince you, and myself, that motives could be found. But we're going at this the wrong way around. All these motives are conceivable, but unless we have some other kind of evidence they are unprovable. No. We'll have to go at it another way."

"Count me in," Michael said firmly.

"Naturally," Jacqueline said. She avoided Jean's eye; and Jean knew what she was thinking. Michael's touching concern for her safety, his exposure of Ted—none of these absolved him from suspicion. Quite the contrary. They were moves a clever man might make in order to win the confidence of his next victim.

SEVEN

W HEN the phone rang next morning, Jean answered it. Jacqueline was still asleep; Jean had the impression that she had been up most of the night, walking and muttering, or simply sitting and staring at the wall while she smoked one cigarette after another.

It was Andy. His greeting made Jean groan.

"Oh, no, Andy. I'd forgotten all about it. I can't. I'm not in the mood for any more subterranean rambles."

"That's silly. Look, Angel, I set this appointment up a month ago. You have to have connections to see this place."

"I don't think I can stand anyone as cheerful as you are this morning," Jean grumbled. "I take it you finished your résumé?"

"Yes. Dropped it off this morning. Come on, babe, I'm celebrating. Jake is coming, isn't she?"

"I don't know. She's still—"

Jean glanced up. Jacqueline stood weaving in the doorway, her face puffed with sleep and her eyes peering blearily through a fine cloud of copper hair. She made violent gestures, and Jean said,

"Wait a second, Andy," and covered the mouthpiece with her hand.

"What's he want?"

"We're supposed to go out to San Sebastiano today, to see some more damned catacombs."

"Oh." Jacqueline's eyes narrowed still further. "Is that where some scholars say Saints Peter and Paul were buried?"

"Yes. How did you know that?"

"Once a librarian, always a librarian. I read." Jacqueline gestured at the telephone, which was emitting frustrated squawks. "Okay, tell him we'll come."

After Jean had hung up, she looked reproachfully at her friend.

"What is this, detective fever or just general curiosity? I don't particularly want to go."

"A little of both," Jacqueline said, ignoring her complaint. "I'm an inveterate sightseer, and this business of saints is obsessing me. It keeps cropping up. . . ."

"You don't think you're going to solve Albert's murder by locating the relics of Saint Peter, do you?"

"There is something," Jacqueline muttered. "Something . . . I've been trying to think."

"So I see." Jean fanned the air ostentatiously. It was still thick with stale smoke; they had taken to locking the place up tightly at night. "I feel like Watson. Remember Holmes's habit of sitting up all night smoking his awful pipes?"

"You'd better let me be Watson, I don't seem to be doing very well as Holmes. Maybe I'm more the Miss Marple type."

"With a figure like yours?"

"My figure is sagging, and so are my brains. After a few more days of this, they'll be running like butter. . . . Where are we meeting the others?"

"At the Colosseum. The Via Appia bus leaves from there."

They took a taxi, since Jacqueline refused to drive in the old city. By the time they reached their destination Jean was beginning to sympathize with Jacqueline's daughter; Jacqueline sang most of the way. Her voice was pleasant and not too loud, and the taxi driver didn't seem to mind; like most taxi drivers, he had already seen everything. But Jean found her friend's repertoire unnerving. It ranged from "Work, for the Night is Coming," to "Smoke Gets in Your Eyes," to a lugubrious German song Jean didn't know.

The bus was crowded; this was a popular, cheap tourist excursion as well as a regular bus route. Pummeled and shoved, Jean collapsed onto the nearest seat. When she had caught her breath and brushed her hair back from her face she was edified to note that Jacqueline had neatly snagged Professor Scoville. He was sitting beside her, his head turned, and a smile on his face as she chatted. Experience counts, Jean thought. She had seen Dana clinging to Scoville's arm as the taxi drove up. Three seats back, across the aisle, Dana was scowling like a thundercloud. Wearing a thin knit sleeveless shirt which displayed her adherence to one of the basic principles of Women's Liberation, and a skirt so short it looked like an apron, she was the center of a circle of admiring eyes.

The others were scattered. Michael and Ann had found seats together; Jean noticed that unlikely combination with interest. The two of them got along amiably enough, but Michael's rampant masculinity clearly made Ann nervous. "She acts like a Christian virgin cornered by Attila the Hun," Michael had complained once. He had been careful not to push her, and now she seemed to be enjoying their conversation. There was a faint flush on her cheeks as she talked.

Andy and José were also sitting together; they were apparently absorbed in one of their interminable arguments. Jean saw José roll his eyes in mock despair as Andy, laughing, made some inaudible point.

Ted was sitting directly across the aisle.

Seeing his familiar face, with its thick glasses and broad smile, Jean was seized by a sensation of unreality. It was impossible, the idea Michael had suggested. . . . Then, juxtaposed to Ted's face, her imagination shaped that other—the face of the falcon girl, as Jacqueline had called her. Michael was right; that face, once seen, could not easily be forgotten.

"Hey." Ted nudged her. "What are you thinking about? Your face has gone blank, like a statue's."

"Oh, nothing much . . ."

"You're not worrying about your report, are you? Forget it for a time. That's over; the die is cast, one way or another."

"That doesn't make me stop worrying," Jean said wryly.

"But it should. Once the deadline is past, or the decision has been made, the worry is useless. To wait for the deadline . . . to make the decision—that's the agonizing part."

"Now you're blanking out," Jean said, forcing her voice to sound casual. She had never seen Ted look quite like that. His face was older, harder.

"Are you American?" The girl sitting next to Jean spoke, and Jean turned to talk to her. No matter how much you might love Rome, it was a pleasure to hear your native language spoken, and a common tongue was introduction enough. She talked to the other girl—a student from an Eastern college, on a summer tour—until Ted nudged her again. It was time to leave the bus.

They were almost the only ones to get off the bus at that stop; most of the travelers were going on, to the better-known catacombs or to a spot farther out in the country from which they could hike back to town, visiting "sights" as they went. The nine of them clustered together, and Andy indicated the building across the narrow road.

"There it is. The basilica of San Sebastiano. One of the seven pilgrimage churches," he added, with a quick glance at Jacqueline. "But we aren't here to visit the church, which, for you ignorant laymen, has little of interest. We have an appointment with Padre Montini, one of the archaeologists in charge of the excavations."

"I am disoriented," José said, looking around. "Ah, no, I see one landmark. That is the tomb of Cecilia Metella, is it not?"

He indicated a gray structure farther down the road.

"Right." Andy nodded. "This is, of course, the Via Appia Antica, the ancient road famed in song and story. It was lined with tombs and cemeteries in ancient times. Almost all of them have been vandalized and carried away now. This is the road Saint Peter took when he copped out during the Neronian persecution, and back that way a piece he met the Saviour and asked the well-known question. There's a church on the spot now—the church of Quo Vadis, Domine. But the best relic of the occasion is here, in San Sebastiano—the footprints of Christ, in the actual rock where he stood."

"Oh," said Ted innocently. "I would very much like to

see that. Can we go into the church?"

"You know very well," said José, "that no one believes—"

Grinning, Andy glanced at his watch.

"We're a little early. I guess we can run quickly around the interior of the basilica. I'd hate to have Moshe miss any relics."

"Moshe?" Jacqueline asked. "I know you all have a passion for nicknames, but—"

"I developed an eye infection the first week I was here," Ted explained soberly.

"Silly joke," Dana muttered. She was still sulking, but at least she was condescending to talk. Jean fell into step with the other girl as they crossed the road and, in an effort to improve her humor, asked,

"Aren't those catacombs we visited out this way somewhere?"

"There are catacombs all over the place," Andy answered, before Dana could speak. "We'll see one set this morning. Possibly the originals. This area was called *catacumbas* in ancient times, so the name came to be applied to the underground cemeteries in the region. That's what catacombs are—burial places. They weren't limited to the Christians, either. There are pagan catacombs and Jewish catacombs—at least four of those have been located, and Ted thinks he may be on the track of another."

"Is that right?" Scoville asked, turning toward Ted with considerable interest. "What material are you using?"

Ted looked as sly as a round-faced, amiable youth could look, and Dana said, with a laugh,

"You ought to know better than to ask another archae-ologist a question like that, Sam."

"He's safe from me," Scoville said, smiling. "If it were an Etruscan cemetery, now . . ."

Glancing over her shoulder, Jean caught a peculiar expression on Jacqueline's face and wondered what, if anything, in the conversation had prompted that look of sudden surmise. She had no opportunity to ask; Andy marshaled them into a group and led the way into the church.

Ted enjoyed the relics thoroughly. The footprints, twice normal size, were such crude fakes that even José was unable to keep a straight face. Chuckling with quiet malice, Ted pointed out an arrow in a glass case. He said nothing, merely raised an eyebrow inquiringly. Glumly, José nodded.

"You know too much about the legends of the saints," he said. "I think you read them only to annoy me. . . . Yes, Sebastian was the saint who was martyred by being shot full of arrows."

"All right, all right, break it up," Andy interposed. "Let's go. We're supposed to meet our guide next door, in the museum."

Padre Montini, wearing a coarse cowled robe and rope belt, was a lean man of middle height with a rugged peasant face. He greeted the girls with broad appreciative smiles, and José with reserve. Scoville got a deep bow and a handclasp that lasted longer than he wanted it to last. The padre knew him by reputation, it seemed.

Montini began by showing them a cleverly constructed model that showed the existing basilica in relationship to its fourth-century predecessor and to the ancient cemetery which had preceded both churches. Andy had already explained that the basilica had not always been named after Saint Sebastian. In the early Christian centuries it had been known as the Church of the Apostles; and the ruins of a Christian cult center, under the church, confirmed the fact that the two great saints were connected in some fashion with the place.

Andy interrupted at this point to ask a question. Jean didn't follow his Italian, which was considerably more fluent than hers; but the effect on Montini was amazing. His face turned bright red and he burst into speech. Scoville Senior backed up his offspring, and the argument raged. Bewildered, Jean turned to José, who stood beside her.

"What's the fight about?"

José grinned.

"Andy asked Montini about the old problem of Saint Peter's daughter. The church holds that the relationship was a purely spiritual one, but Andy is insisting that Petronella was the Apostle's physical child."

Jacqueline joined them in time to hear the question and José's answer.

"Doesn't the Bible mention Peter's wife?"

"I believe so," José said indifferently. "It is not a question of great importance."

Jacqueline shook her head, muttering. Jean caught a few words; they sounded like "another virgin saint."

Finally the disputants calmed down, and Montini announced,

"And now, *andiamo! Discendiamo nel sotterraneo!*"

Jean looked at Michael, and met a cold glare. Apparently he was still climbing back on the horse that had thrown him. After seeing the condition he had been in once before *"nel sotterraneo,"* she wasn't sure this trip was a good idea.

Fifteen minutes later she was sure that it wasn't a good idea. They had visited catacombs before, and she had not liked them much; for an atmosphere of pure concentrated gloom there is no place worse than the corridor of a catacomb. These were even more depressing than the others she had visited. Some of the more popular catacombs, often visited by tourists, had a feeble lighting system. Here the group walked in single file, holding candles as the sole source of illumination. The corridors were so narrow that the bigger men—Scoville, Andy, and José—had to turn sideways in some places. The low ceiling was only inches over their heads. And on either side, yard after yard and block after block, the grave niches filled the walls from floor to ceiling—tiers of graves, row on row on row, stretching out into the darkness eternally.

Jean wondered how on earth Michael could stand it. Had he been joking about his claustrophobia—inventing it, to explain a distress which might have had another cause? Jean wondered. She couldn't imagine how anyone who had found San Clemente disturbing could endure this place.

Half the candles had gone out, as the result of incautious movements on the part of the bearers. From the head of the procession Montini called out a cheery reassurance. They were not to worry, he could find his way through this maze blindfolded.

Jean found the statement unconvincing. People had been lost in the catacombs; the corridors had no regular plan, they branched and intersected at random. There were no landmarks, only the same grimly monotonous walls and their blocked-up niches. A few of the graves had been opened; the gaping blackness within held shadowy suggestions of what had once inhabited the space. Occasionally there was an inscription or a sketchy drawing on the plaster that sealed the grave. Montini's voice echoed hollowly as he pointed out some of the symbols—the dove, the fish, the olive branch, other emblems of the Faith—and the rare epitaphs. "Be of good cheer; no man is immortal," one read, with a Spartan fortitude that struck Jean as more pagan than Christian. The most common epitaph was the simple phrase "in peace."

They might have been a funeral procession from the time when the catacombs were still in use. The roughness of the floor necessitated a funereal shuffle; the dim light illumined faces that seemed drawn and anxiously shadowed, leaving the rest of the figures in darkness. Gradually an unholy fascination replaced Jean's nervousness. She kept stopping to stare at the mute shapes of the graves, morbidly picturing what lay within them. She was at the end of the line, and there was a tendency on the part of the others to crowd forward, close to the comforting figure of their guide. They were silent. Even Montini had stopped talking. The atmosphere discouraged speech. All at once Jean looked up from her contemplation of a very small niche, whose miniature dimensions had struck her poignantly, and found that she was alone.

She strained her eyes through the enclosing darkness and tried to deny the fact. It was impossible. They had to be here, they couldn't simply disappear. . . . From somewhere seemingly an immense distance away there was a hollow echo of a voice, or a laugh.

Jean took three quick running steps and stubbed her toe on a protruding stone. The small yellow candle flame flickered wildly. Gasping with terror, Jean sheltered it with her hand. If that light went out she was done for. "The horror of the darkness . . ." It was Saint Jerome who had said that. He must have known it himself—not the ordinary lightlessness of night, but the darkness of death and the grave.

Jean knew it would be folly to move. She was completely disoriented, and there were branching corridors every few yards. Sooner or later they would miss her, and Montini, who presumably knew where he had been, as well as where he was going, would retrace the path to look for her. If she stayed where she was, she was safe. . . .

The word suddenly struck her with a new and terrible meaning. Safe from abandonment she certainly would be, unless she panicked; but if her theories were correct, another danger had been haunting her footsteps for many days. Was this episode to be a fourth, and final, "accident?"

When she heard a sound, she started violently. Magnified and distorted, it sounded more like a howl than a name, but as soon as she steadied herself, and her precious candle, she realized that it was a name—hers. The sound demolished what few wits she had remaining. She began to run—whether toward a rescuer or away from a faceless killer she did not know—and plunged headlong into an approaching figure. Her candle went out, which was fortunate, since otherwise it would have ignited the man's shirt. He saved his own candle by a complicated last-minute stretch, and caught her in his free arm.

"Michael," Jean whispered.

"Undeniably. What's with you? Why all the panic?"

"You're a fine one to ask that." Jean stepped back, and he let her go at once. "Are you—are you all right?"

"Who, me? Fine." He smiled. "I'm cured. I'm even getting to like this."

"I'm not." There was something else she didn't like; the look on Michael's face and the way his eyes shone in the candlelight. They looked solid, the pupils greatly dilated. With his faint, enigmatic smile, it was an unnerving expression.

"Now that you've been good enough to rescue me, let's join the others," she said.

"Why? It's nice and quiet here. This is the way it was supposed to be. No wisecracking sightseers, gaping and pretending to be frightened . . ."

"Michael—"

"I haven't been to mass since I was thirteen," Michael went on, in a dreamy voice. "I was so turned off I couldn't pass by a church without spitting. And the Jesus movement never got to me, I don't dig that kind of exhibitionism. But in a place like this you begin to see what they were driving at. The meaning behind the symbols; the fact that two opposites don't clash, but resolve into a synthesis. Death and resurrection; the body back to the dust it came from, and the soul to God."

"Michael," Jean repeated. She had to fight an insane instinct to shout, as if she were calling him back from a great distance. "Please. You're frightening me."

"What are you frightened of? They'll find us soon. Unless we move—back that way. . . ."

Jean decided she was going to scream. She didn't want to; surely she must be imagining the pressure of Michael's body against hers, forcing her back into one of those dark side corridors. Even so, she was going to scream.

She opened her mouth—and Andy came plunging around a turn in the passage. He was holding his candle high, and the light made his mop of hair glow like a nimbus.

"All right, sorry to break it up," he said coolly. "But Montini is having fits. He's been telling us gruesome stories of people who got lost down here and weren't found for years and years and . . . So suppose you find a more appropriate place, hmm?"

"Anytime I pick a place like this to make out you can have my head examined," Michael said, in his normal voice. "We were merely exchanging philosophical comments. Lead on, you louse."

The others were waiting for them in a tiny rough-walled chapel. Montini burst into agitated speech when they came in. When he had finished his scolding and the procession moved on, Jean managed to slip in next to Jacqueline.

"Sorry," she said, under her breath. "I don't know how that happened. Do you think . . ."

"I don't think so. But—for God's sake, stick close."

Almost immediately they came out of the dismal corridors into an open underground space. It was roofed by a complex system of ancient beams and modern girders, and Jean realized, before their guide spoke, that they were now under the church. Two different ages of history were represented by the structures in that open area. There was a row of Roman mausolea in front of them, neat little brick houses whose pointed facades looked as if they had been built within the past decade. Off to one side were the remaining walls of the Christian cult center, which had been constructed over the street of tombs two or three centuries later.

Montini began explaining the layout, and Jean stopped listening. She really didn't care whether Peter and Paul had been buried at all, much less where. Michael had had a point, even though she didn't think he had chosen a good time or place for his theological musings. The body went back to the dust; physical relics were only trinkets, like the pebbles or shells collected by a child as mementos of a trip. Wasn't it Paul himself who had said, "But when I became a man, I put away childish things"?

Yet she could understand the appeal made by those worthless remnants of mortality. The soul was so barricaded by flesh that it needed concrete objects to cling to. Squatting down under the low eaves of the church floor above, Jean felt a sympathetic quiver run through her as she viewed the graffiti scratched onto the wall by the men and women who had come to pray near the bones of the Apostles.

"*Paule et Petre, petite pro Victore*," she read aloud; and Jacqueline, squatting beside her, translated.

"Peter and Paul, pray for Victor. How do you like that?

I do remember a little Latin from twenty years ago."

"Very good," said Andy, behind them. "Ignore Jean's accent, though, she's a medieval Latinist, and the way she pronounces the language sets my teeth on edge."

"I'd better keep my mouth shut, then," Jacqueline said, pushing her glasses back into place. "I keep forgetting that most of you know Latin as well as you do English."

"It's a working language for us," Andy agreed. "All right, girls, tear yourselves away. Time for some pagan tombs."

The others were on the lower level, in front of the mausolea. Over one brick facade a marble plaque still remained in place, recording the name of the man to whom the tomb had belonged. With the others egging her on, Jacqueline tried to translate the inscription. She was having a fine time; her hair was coming loose, and her glasses kept sliding down her nose.

"I can't even get the first word," she complained. "MCL—is that a date?"

"*M* for Marcus," Andy said. "Marcus Clodius Hermes—that was the guy's name."

"Oh. I see. 'Marcus Clodius Hermes, who'—I've got it! 'Who lived . . . years . . .' Now that is a number. Wait a minute, I always have to count Roman numerals on my fingers. 'Who lived seventy-five years . . .' "

Her voice died away. Dana laughed and prompted her; but Andy, more perceptive, reached out and caught her arm.

"Jake, what's the matter?"

Jacqueline turned. The sight of her face made Jean recoil. It was white as paper, with two bright spots of color burning on her cheeks. Coils of loosened bronze hair curled around her ears like copper ornaments. She paid no attention to Andy, or to the others, but broke through them, brushing them aside as if she were brushing at flies.

She caught Jean by the shoulders and shook her. Jean was too astonished to resist. Her head bobbed back and forth.

"You overeducated brats and your damned erudition," Jacqueline said, literally between clenched teeth. "Here. Paper. Pen. I've got one here someplace. . . ." She rummaged frantically in the purse, like a puppy in pursuit of a gopher. "Hell, take my eyebrow pencil." She shoved it into Jean's limp hand. "Write. Write down what you saw Albert write. Go on! Exactly what he wrote."

Even then Jean couldn't understand what she was getting at. But she did as she was told; and as the strokes emerged, smudged and dark, they had an unnerving resemblance to the uneven strokes Albert's finger had made. Jacqueline snatched the pad and waved it in the air.

"I thought so," she exclaimed. "How we could have been so stupid. . . . Not the number—the numeral! The Roman numeral seven."

EIGHT

A CHASTENED Jacqueline was led, gently but firmly, across the street to the bus stop. She was still muttering to herself. Padre Montini, who had been vexed by Jean's adventure, found Jacqueline's outburst the final straw. He was glad to bid them all farewell and retire to his pasta.

The others knew what Jacqueline was talking about, but Dana voiced their mutual feelings when she said she couldn't understand what the flap was all about.

"What difference does it make? A seven is a seven whether it's a Roman or an Arabic numeral."

There was a soft-drink stand in the shady parking lot across from the church, and after their tramp through the dusty centuries they were all glad for a drink. They stood around sucking soda pop through straws like a party of Scouts on an outing. Andy said thoughtfully,

"It does make a difference. It provides a context."

Jacqueline, drinking Coke with such concentration that her cheeks were concave and her eyes practically crossed, looked at him.

"You're a bright lad, Andy. Jean, why didn't you—"

"I'm stupid," Jean admitted. "But as Andy said, we all think in Latin half the time. Every contemporary document I refer to is written in Latin—manuscripts, inscriptions, everything. Even graffiti. I'm so used to seeing it. . . ."

"I know. I'm sorry I yelled at you. Was I awfully rude?"

"As invective," Andy said meditatively, "it was pretty feeble. But it had a familiar ring."

"Stop it, Junior," said his father, affectionately but firmly. "Haven't I taught you to be polite to a lady?"

"Jacqueline is not a lady," said Ted. He smiled at her. "She is one of us."

Jean felt a chill run up her spine. Before Ted's smiling regard, Jacqueline changed color and looked away.

They split up after that, the majority of them returning to the Institute. José had a sketch he wanted to finish, and Andy admitted that he could spend a few hours working without actually hurting himself. Ted said nothing about his plans. When the bus disgorged them beside the Colosseum he simply removed himself, smiling affably, and strolled away down the Via dei Fori Imperiali.

Turning, Jean met Michael's eye, and knew what he was thinking. Ted had taken the shortest way to the Piazza Colonna.

Jean went to the library with the others, but she was unable to concentrate. Instead she sat and doodled idly on a piece of paper. There were a few people in the reading room at that time, the drowsy, warm, post-lunch hour. The three art students had gone to their studios and Andy had retired to his private cubicle in the stacks. The sunlight pouring in the big windows made Jean sleepy. She drew stiff Byzantine figures across the pages of her notebook, and brooded.

After all the excitement of Jacqueline's discovery, she couldn't see that they had progressed. What difference did it make whether Albert's last message was in Latin or Arabic numerals? Andy had said something about the context. Jean understood; like the others who worked with Latin, Albert would be more inclined to use that numbering system if the subject uppermost in his mind related to things Roman. Which meant precisely nothing. Saints, hills, churches, many of the other exotic ideas they had considered were "Roman" subjects. None of these subjects had offered any fruitful ideas to begin with, and they still didn't.

Jean groaned, and regarded her drawing with disfavor. Unconsciously she had been sketching a mosaic from one of the Ravenna churches—a long line of lady saints, more or less identical except for the symbols that distinguished one from the other. Saint Agnes and her lamp, Saint Catherine and her wheel, Saint Barbara and her tower . . .

Could there be some meaning in Albert's raving about his virgin saints? Iconography was one of the fields she had to know, since the saints and their symbols were a favorite theme in medieval mosaics. There weren't seven virgin saints, there were thousands of those unfortunate females, counting Saint Ursula of Cologne and her thousand fellow-sufferers. But suppose Albert hadn't been thinking about German saints or Armenian saints or French saints. The Roman saints and their churches; could anything be made of that?

A fly buzzed by and settled on her paper. Jean swatted at it, and missed; she hadn't meant to hit it anyway. She was getting sleepy, the droning fly and the hot sun acted like sedatives. Virgin saints and Roman churches. It would make a good title for a book, a popular book on early Christian archaeology.

That was all the sense it made, though. Jacqueline wasn't too communicative these days, but she had already considered this equation, and Jean assumed she had derived nothing meaningful from it. Their expeditions to Santa Cecilia and the other churches dedicated to virgin saints had produced no comment from Jacqueline; in fact, Jean had wondered at the time if the sightseeing was only an excuse for conversation with various Sinners.

There was one consoling feature in their discovery of that morning. It was unlikely that Albert would think of his seven acquaintances in terms of Roman numerals. The Seven Sinners . . . She cursed Andy for inventing that unoriginal name. . . .

"Hey," Andy said in her ear. "If you're going to sleep you might as well do it in a bed."

"I wasn't asleep." Jean rubbed her eyes. "Not very asleep . . . This place is getting hotter by the minute."

"It's even hotter back in the stacks. How about a swim?"

"All the way to Ostia? I haven't got the strength."

"Maybe Jake would let us use her pool. We wouldn't need to bother her. Oh, cripes," Andy said. "I forgot. Maybe you don't feel like swimming."

"Sure I do," Jean said, with more bravado than truth. "I don't think Jacqueline would mind. Let's go ask the others."

The others were only too glad to leave their sweltering studios. José was the only holdout; barely glancing up from his easel, he informed them that he almost had it, and if they would get their worthless carcasses out of there he just might get it. All right, all right—he would meet them later for dinner, he would do anything they wanted—later. But now, would they please get out?

They left, unoffended; all of them had been through that stage themselves.

The quickest way to their goal was along the old Via Aurelia, which Jean had traveled once at night, by car. It was a hot, dusty walk, and by the time they reached the back entrance to the compound where Jacqueline lived, they were all panting. Jean had shared the apartment for a week now and had her own key; she led the way upstairs without a second thought. She did caution the others to be quiet. Jacqueline might be taking a nap, since she had expected to be alone all afternoon.

But when they stepped out of the elevator, Jean realized that Jacqueline was not asleep. Nor was she alone. A few breathless words and an odd scuffling sound from the *salone* alarmed her; she darted forward, followed by the others. Then she stopped, staring.

On the couch that faced the foyer, Jacqueline was disentangling herself from her visitor. She was flushed and disheveled. Her companion looked familiar to Jean. Tall, suave, distinguished, elegantly dressed in a pale tan suit and dark shirt . . .

"Lieutenant," said Jean, her voice rising to a squeak.

"Signorina," said di Cavallo resignedly. "And"—his voice became a snarl—"signori, signorina. . . . Are there more of you? I see, Signora Kirby, that you are *molto occupata.*"

"Too busy for that," Jacqueline said, closing her mouth with the snap of a trapdoor shutting. "I must say, Lieutenant, that your behavior—"

"Enough," said di Cavallo, bounding to his feet. "We have no more to say to one another. It is finished. *Buona sera, signora. Arrivederla.*"

Regrettably, Jean found this amusing. *Arrivederla* is the formal version of the Italian word for "good-bye," which Americans use so casually and inaccurately. *Arrivederci* is properly applied only to intimates, children, dogs, and the Almighty—should one ever have occasion to say

"Good-bye, God"—and di Cavallo was quite correct in using the formal word to address a lady who had resolutely indicated her intention of avoiding informal relations. It sounded funny, all the same, when Jean remembered her first sight of the couple. To complete her demoralization, she caught sight of a small fuzzy pink head poking out from under the brocaded flounce of the couch. Prinz looked apologetic, as well he might; as a watchdog he wasn't very courageous.

Di Cavallo saw Jean's grin, and his handsome face froze into a mask of fury. Looking six inches taller than his actual height, he stalked toward the elevator. There was an unseemly melee in the foyer; the other invaders had retreated precipitately as soon as they realized what was going on, and they were milling in an uncertain group near the door. Finally di Cavallo managed to reach the elevator. He entered it, and stood with his back to them until the door closed.

Meeting Jean's eye, Andy twisted his features into a grimace of amused chagrin. She made a reassuring gesture and advanced tentatively into the *salone.*

Jacqueline, smoothing down her ruffled hair, said coolly, "You may as well come in. All of you."

"I'm sorry," Jean began.

"You'd be within your rights to blast us," Andy added. "We had no business barging in here."

"Dear boy, don't apologize. Who knows," Jacqueline said dreamily, "what you may have saved me from? A fate—"

"I'd prefer that to death any day," said Ann. "What did he come here for, Jake?"

"Hey, babe," Andy said, staring at his sister in surprise. "Watch it."

"That's all right," Jacqueline said. "He dropped by to give me the latest results of the investigation. The police seem to assume I'm the adult responsible for this group of nuts. Sorry about that."

"We're sorry you were dragged into it," Andy said, still glaring at his sister. "You've been damned nice, and the only reward we seem to offer you is involvement in our messy private affairs. Am I right in supposing the lieutenant was only using that as an excuse to—er—call on you?"

"I refuse to answer on the usual grounds. Anyhow, the suicide-theory stands. I imagine that's something of a relief."

She looked at them inquiringly. It was Andy who answered.

"Not really. I don't know about the rest of you guys, but I haven't thought much about it. That sounds callous, I suppose, but—well, there wasn't much doubt, was there?"

"At any rate, it's over and done with," Jacqueline said. "And," she added casually, "so is my visit to Rome almost over. Lise is returning on Sunday, and my work here is done. So I'll be leaving."

"Oh, no," Andy said. "You can't leave us like this. What are we going to do without our mother image? And her swimming pool?"

"You'll have to return to your slummy, poverty-stricken existence," Jacqueline said nastily. "That's the trouble with giving you long-haired degenerates a few comforts;

you get so you expect them. When you're my age, you'll appreciate the value of hard work and a set of decent moral values. I don't know what this generation is coming to. Immoral, shiftless, pot-smoking. . . . Ann, darling, don't look like that. I'm joking."

Ann's sober face lightened. She glanced uncertainly from one grinning face to the next; and Andy said cheerfully, "Jake's just getting back into practice. That's the way she talks to students when she's on duty."

Jean managed to produce a smile, but she felt as if someone had kicked her in the pit of the stomach. Fond as she was of Jacqueline, it wasn't the loss of the mother image, as Andy had called her, that bothered Jean; it was Jacqueline's change of attitude. No one with any sense of compassion or responsibility could walk out on an unsolved murder and a very vulnerable witness; and Jacqueline was not lacking in either trait. What had di Cavallo told her, before his hormones got the better of him? Jean tried to be rational. If Jacqueline had become convinced that their murder theory was baseless—and no other theory could explain her readiness to withdraw— then there was nothing for Jean to worry about. Her mind believed it, but every nerve in her body howled in protest.

"I'll move out today," she said. "I never meant to stay so long."

"Jean," Ann said hesitantly. "You did have a bad shock. If you're still nervous about being alone, Andy and I would love to have you."

"Especially Andy," said that gentleman, with a hideous leer. "No, seriously, honey—Ann is right. You don't realize how long the effects of shock can last. I know. It happened to Ann once. Suicide—a friend of ours. She went along cool as a cucumber for a couple of months, and then, whammo; it hit her. She was out of this world for a long time."

Jean didn't dare look at Ann. The other girl had never referred to this incident, and Jean couldn't help resenting Andy's mention of it now, even though his motive for doing so was kind. Ann rallied quickly. She had made one sharp, uncontrolled motion of protest; now she said quietly,

"He's right, Jean. Though maybe you don't feel like moving in now, with a—a crazy woman."

"Don't put on airs," Michael said, before Andy could protest. "You aren't the only one."

"To have a friend kill himself?"

"Oh, that. Look, honey, they fall like flies in my profession. Unstable artists, you know. No, I mean you aren't the only one who's spent time on some shrink's couch. It's the in thing nowadays. We're all a little crazy, one way or the other. Hadn't you noticed?"

"There's no need for Jean to make up her mind right this minute," Jacqueline said. "You might as well wait till Sunday, Jean, and move out when I do. Anyway, you can't leave before tomorrow. I'm having a party. A farewell party, for me."

"Great," Andy said heartily. "When, tomorrow night? Are we all invited?"

"Naturally. Spread the word to the others, will you?"

"Can I bring my daddy?" Andy asked, in a plaintive squawk.

"I hope you will. It's a costume party. Will Dr. Scoville mind?"

"He's the biggest ham in Europe. Where do you think I get it? He'll probably want to come as a Pharaoh; that's his favorite disguise. Gives him a chance to show off his muscles."

"But I don't think we have—" Ann began.

"I'll think of something," her brother waved her objections aside. "It'll be a surprise."

"Surprise," Jacqueline repeated. She bent over and began to rummage in the purse, which squatted on the floor at her feet. But Jean had seen her face before she moved to hide it, and its sudden pallor told the younger woman all she needed to know. The conversation, the party, di Cavallo's visit—all were part of a larger plan. And the consummation of that plan appalled even the woman who had arranged it.

Jacqueline didn't join them at the pool, but she sat on the balcony watching every move they made. Jean hadn't been aware of apprehension; but when the actual moment of entering the water came, it took all her will-power to make her body comply. She paddled sedately around the edge, in full view of the balcony, and everyone carefully refrained from commenting on her caution.

They left Jacqueline preparing to go out. Jean wondered with whom she was dining, but of course did not ask. They had been selfish, assuming she had no other friends in Rome.

Their own dinner was a quiet affair. Everyone seemed subdued, and when José joined them, to be informed of Jacqueline's plans, he received the news with a silent shrug. Somewhat to Jean's surprise, the idea of a costume party seemed to please him.

"I am thinking," he said, pressing his fingertips to his temples. "I will invent something."

"Why don't you come as Torquemada?" Andy asked. "That would be in character."

Under cover of the ensuing argument, Jean turned to Michael. He was back to his sketching again. She tried to see what he was doing, but he shook his head and moved the book away.

"Wait till it's finished."

"What costume are you going to wear?" Jean asked.

"Dunno."

"Don't shave tomorrow," Andy advised. "Then you can come as a Skid Row bum. In your usual clothes, of course."

"You're even more vicious than usual tonight," Jean said admiringly.

"Mike's sartorial tastes have always offended me," was the reply.

Michael glanced up from his sketch to survey his friend with contempt.

"Anybody who would wear a pink flowered shirt and a string of blue love beads has got no business criticizing my clothes."

"What about me?" Jean asked, to avert another uproar. "You haven't made any suggestions for me."

Andy's face softened as he looked at her.

"Come as a saint," he said. "Almost any saint would do."

Michael made an odd choking sound.

They broke up early, by mutual consent. José had some complex scheme for a costume, which demanded immediate action, and the others planned to track down Ted and Dana, to tell them about the party. Jean had been hoping they would go their respective ways before she made her move; but they lingered, and finally she was forced to action. She hailed a taxi.

Andy greeted this gesture with rude comments about the rich and the rich by association. Jean's retorts were weak, but this was one promise, made to Jacqueline, that she intended to keep.

Michael closed the taxi door for her. As he withdrew, Jean felt something flutter down into her lap. The sheet of paper had been folded several times, but she knew it must be one of Michael's sketches. The light was poor, so she didn't try to look at it.

It was still early; Jacqueline would not be back from a conventional dinner for some time yet. But as Jean nerved herself for the entrance into a darkened hall, she realized that the apartment was not deserted. The foyer was lit, and there were sounds from the kitchen. She hesitated, holding the elevator door open. Then footsteps shuffled down the hall. Jacqueline's appearance matched her dispirited shuffle. She was wearing a faded cotton robe and her face had sagged into weary lines. Jean stepped out and let the door close.

"What are you doing back so early?"

"It was a business dinner," Jacqueline said, with an odd twist of her mouth. "You took a cab?"

"Yes. Are you going to tell me what's going on?"

Jacqueline dropped into a chair.

"I don't think I'd better," she said.

Jean sat down, and the poodle came trotting across the

floor and flung himself down on her feet. The French doors to the balcony were open; a breeze drifted in, bringing with it the scent of pines and the soft sea-sound which was the rustle of branches in the wind. The sounds and smells and sensations blended into a unique whole which would always recall these Italian nights, just as the sun on a hot street lined with old houses would always summon up the nostalgia of Rome on a summer day. I don't want to lose this, Jean thought. And I will; it will be lost in nightmares unless . . .

"Then you haven't changed your mind," she said. "About Albert's death."

"No. Did you think I was running out on you? I ought to be insulted."

"I didn't really think that. In fact, I wondered whether the lieutenant's visit might not be more than coincidental."

"Look," Jacqueline said wearily. "I'm not being mysterious for the fun of it. There are reasons. Just don't worry. You'll be all right. . . . What's this?"

"One of Michael's sketches, I think. He gave it to me tonight."

Jacqueline raised an inquiring eyebrow and Jean nodded. Jacqueline spread the paper out on the coffee table. The sudden tension of her shoulders roused Jean's curiosity. She leaned over to see the sketch.

It was brilliant, one of the best things Michael had ever done—and one of the most terrifying. It was done in a manner quite different from his usual broad, quick technique; the figures were small, the detail precise. And it stopped Jean's breath for a moment, because the subject was so similar to the one she had been sketching that day.

Like hers, Michael's drawing showed a row of stiff Byzantine saints. Or—Sinners? There were seven of them. The faces were exquisite little portraits, but it was the detail of costume and symbol that made Jean start to wonder.

As people will, she looked first at herself. Her initial reaction was pleasure; Michael had flattered her, it was a lovely little face, heart-shaped, smiling her own triangular smile. He had shown her as Saint Agnes, with a lamb at her feet. . . . Jean straightened up, with a snort of mingled amusement and fury. The lamb had her face too. Even when she studied it closely she couldn't see how Michael had managed it; the face was that of a juvenile sheep, muzzle, ears and all, and yet it was immediately recognizable as her own.

Dana was Mary Magdalene. The subject was more popular in Renaissance art, with its fondness for the naked body, but Michael had produced a wonderful satire of the stiff Byzantine style, with long, stylized waves of hair that exposed more than they concealed, and the false modesty of the fat little hands.

Ann was another virgin saint. Michael had dealt kindly with her—or at least Jean thought he had until she examined the face more closely. It was a face suited to a saint who died a martyr; there were lines of torment under its seeming placidity. Jean had to find the symbol before she could identify the lady. It was Saint Barbara, carrying the tower in which her wicked father had imprisoned her before turning her over to the torturers as a recalcitrant Christian.

The armor and the lance with its dripping dragon's head identified Andy as the handsome Saint George. Did Michael really see him as a dragon slayer? Ted made a charming Saint Stephen; he had caught the first rock in his upraised hand, and his look of supercilious superiority would have driven any mob to stone him.

José was harder to identify. He wore a bishop's robes and miter, but the higher ecclesiastical ranks have produced a good many saints. However, his expression of studious concentration and the book he carried enabled Jean to recognize Saint Augustine—who had once remarked, "Lord, give me chastity—but not yet." That was really too bad of Michael. The eyes under José's studious brow held a gleam that belonged to the pre-conversion part of Augustine's career.

Bringing up the tail of the procession came Michael's drawing of himself, and after her first chuckle of laughter Jean's mouth curved down, and she forgave him his casual digs at the others. Emaciated, hideous, wild-eyed, it was the ugliest representation of John the Baptist Jean had ever seen. The ribs stood out and the ragged hair framed a face only one step removed from madness.

The Seven Sinners made up the procession, but there were two other figures hovering in the background. Jean glanced at Jacqueline. To date, her hostess had demonstrated no particular religious sensitivities, but the figure with Jacqueline's face might have been considered slightly blasphemous. The flowing hair framed a face which was neither virginal nor motherly—at least not in the sense of that Ideal Motherhood the figure was supposed to exemplify. Jean had seen such a look on her own mother's face, however, under circumstances she did not care to dwell upon. The figure wore a crown; it was tipped over one ear, and the halo was distinctly ragged.

With trepidation, Jean looked to see what Michael had done with Scoville. Some lingering remnant of piety had kept him from casting that gentleman in either of the obvious roles—or else he did not see Scoville as exemplifying divinity. At first Jean couldn't decide what the professor was supposed to be, other than a Roman gentleman in a neatly draped toga. Then she saw what was poking out from under the skirt of the toga, and examined the shape of the curls on the figure's forehead more closely, and again she gasped. That was going too far. Scoville might be a sinner, like all the rest, but to make him the Prince of sinners was an exaggeration.

"The boy is fantastic," Jacqueline muttered. "I've never seen his serious work, but he could win a lot of prizes with this sort of thing."

"It's cruel," Jean said.

"So was Hogarth. So was Daumier."

"You think he's that good?"

"Good Lord, yes. It needs more than technical skill. The great caricaturists have a touch of extrasensory perception. They see through people."

"He does that. Though I don't understand some of these. Yours—you don't mind—"

"It makes me writhe," Jacqueline said. "I didn't think I was that transparent. What about yours?"

"I think it's funny," Jean admitted. "But I don't get it. Or, if I do get it, I'm mad."

"There are worse things than being thought of as a

woolly lamb. Hang on to this, Jean. Or—let me keep it for you. May I?"

"You can have it," Jean said. "As a souvenir."

Jacqueline shivered.

"I think I'd prefer a bright brass paperweight in the shape of St. Peter's. Or a cerise satin pillow with '*Arrivederci Roma*' embroidered on it. Something bland and meaningless."

"I know," Jean said wearily. "It hasn't been pleasant for—" Her voice broke off, and she looked at the drawing with aroused interest. "Are you saying that this sketch means—"

"I'm not saying anything else. I'm too incoherent." Jacqueline rose; and Jean noticed that she held the drawing by its edge, as if it were hot to the touch. "Let's get some sleep. Believe me, we're going to need it."

NINE

THE day of the party dawned bright and clear and hot. The close air woke Jean at sunrise; she kicked off the sheet that had covered her and moved her sweating body to a cooler spot, dislodging Nefertiti, whose affectionate position under her knees had not reduced the temperature. The cat arose, cursing, and removed itself. Jean looked at the other bed. The covers were thrown back, but Jacqueline was not there.

She fell asleep again, too tired to do more than wonder briefly; and when she finally woke again the sun was high and the room was even hotter. The shutters were closed;

bright parallel streaks of light crossed the gloom.

Jean staggered out into the *salone,* which was brighter and not quite so hot. She found Jacqueline fully dressed, drinking coffee. The efficient professional was in command again; Jacqueline's eyes were sunken, as if she hadn't slept well, but her mouth was tightly set and her glasses rode high on the bridge of her nose.

"You have a somewhat haggard aspect," said Jacqueline critically. "Didn't you sleep well?"

"I had a bad dream," Jean said. She shuddered. "Really bad. I'm still shaking."

"Here, have some coffee. What was it about?"

"I dreamed I met Saint Agnes," Jean said, accepting the proffered cup. "Walking down the Via Nomentana."

"The Via—"

"Nomentana. That's the street her church is on, the one outside the walls. I knew it was the Nomentana, even though it looked completely different from the way it looks now. It was like a country road instead of a street, and it was paved with those big dark stone blocks, like the ones you can still see in sections of the Via Appia Antica. There were trees lining the way—dark, pointed cypresses, and pines, and mimosa. Trees and tombs. Some of them were brick mausolea and some were big, elaborate white marble buildings. And then she—she came up out of a stairway that went down into the ground. Like the entrance to the catacombs." Jean sipped her coffee. She said in a small voice, "She was carrying her head under her arm."

"You have an accurate imagination," Jacqueline said. "She was beheaded, wasn't she? You know where you received the stimulus for this—"

"Sure, I know. Damn Michael and his sketches . . . But you know how nightmares are, this was much worse than it sounds when I describe it; when I was dreaming it I was absolutely paralyzed with terror. She wasn't horrible-looking, I mean, there wasn't even any blood. In a way, that would have been better. She—the head—smiled at me. And winked one eye."

"That's enough," Jacqueline said hastily.

"I know it doesn't sound—"

"It sounds ghastly. Forget it. We've got a lot to do. Grocery shopping, cooking, cleaning—and somehow we've got to invent a couple of costumes."

From then on Jean didn't have time to brood—or ask questions. The entire apartment had to be cleaned, and that meant floor scrubbing, waxing, and so on. Jacqueline admitted blandly that she hadn't done much cleaning, and since her friend's *tuttofare* was also on vacation, the apartment had gotten into a state which a persnickety Swiss lady would rightfully resent. It must be spotless before Lise returned, and though some of the work would have to be done over again, after the party, the hard-core cleaning might as well be done at once.

By midafternoon they had finished most of the work, including the manufacture of what seemed to Jean's weary fingers to be thousands of dainty little hors d'oeuvres. She was preparing to collapse when Jacqueline reminded her that they had done nothing about costumes.

Jean's response was profane.

"I have to have one," Jacqueline pointed out. "It was my idea, after all."

"I can't imagine what made you think of such a thing," Jean groaned. "Can't we do something with a bed sheet? A nice toga, maybe."

"Not with Lise's sheets we can't. Have you ever tried to turn a bed sheet into anything resembling human garb of any period? I have been concocting Hallowe'en costumes for longer than you've been alive, and believe me, the easiest thing to do is go to the nearest five-and-ten and buy one. Come along."

Still protesting, Jean was carried off. In a local branch of CIM, the most popular Roman department store, they found a section devoted to folk art and souvenirs. Jean looked dubiously at a shelf of pillows which said "*Arrivederci Roma.*"

"What did you have in mind?" she asked.

"You can be a gondolier," Jacqueline said, picking up a straw hat with a bright crimson streamer down the back. "You've got blue slacks; all you need is the hat and one of those red-and-white striped jerseys."

"Okay, I'll take anything. What about you? You could be the Virgin." Jean indicated a counter where cloth was sold. "Ten yards of that blue . . ."

"I've done that. In fourth grade, in the Christmas play. I'm afraid the part doesn't suit me any longer."

"How about Lady Godiva? It's a shame to waste that hair. Or Rapunzel."

"It's a pity," Jacqueline said regretfully, "that only saints, fairy-tale heroines, and the cast of *Hair* wear their tresses long and flowing. Oh, the hell with it. Let's get some cheesecloth and I'll drape a toga, or the female equivalent. Lise must have some books that show how to do it."

There were books, but they showed only the finished product, and by the time the two had Jacqueline's *palla*—the female equivalent—draped to their satisfaction, they were both helpless with laughter. The effect was good, though, and Jacqueline's red-gold coronet made her look quite imperial. They were trying to decide which empress she ought to be when the buzzer sounded. The first guests had arrived.

There were three of them; the Scovilles had come *en famille*. Professor Scoville, wearing a raincoat and a sheepish expression, demanded a room in which to change. When he reappeared, Andy caught Jean's eye and gave her a broad wink. Scoville, as predicted, had come as an Egyptian Pharaoh. The wide jeweled collar showed off his broad chest and shoulders, and the short tunic bared legs which, if rather hairy, were neither spindly nor shapeless.

Ann and Andy had come as their namesakes, the famous Raggedy twins. Jean fancied that even in Rome, which is accustomed to fantastic garb, they must have aroused considerable attention on the way over. That wouldn't bother Andy, but Jean wondered how he had persuaded his sister to appear in public with Raggedy Ann's bright-painted face.

"With our hair it was inevitable," Andy explained, rumpling his sister's bright mop. "We don't even need wigs."

The others came before long, and it was amusing to see what costumes they had chosen. Michael had taken Andy's cheerful insult literally; his beard was heavy anyway and by letting it go he had achieved a desperately unkempt look. He carried a half-empty jug of wine and seemed to feel that that was all he needed for a complete disguise.

José was Montezuma, complete with (imitation) feathered cape. He refused to explain where he had procured the costume, but it was magnificent. Ted, who had dug out a doublet and tights from a friend's amateur theatrical collection, promptly decided that he was Cortes. With a borrowed eyebrow pencil he drew himself a black Spanish moustache, and went off arm in arm with the Aztec ruler.

Jean expected that Dana would be the last to arrive, and she had anticipated that Dana's costume would be sexy and insubstantial. What she had not expected was that Dana would bring a date.

"I knew you wouldn't mind," she cooed, giving Jacqueline a triumphant glance. "You all remember Giovanni, don't you?"

She was, of course, Cleopatra. And her Mark Antony was Lieutenant di Cavallo.

His appearance cast a momentary pall on the company. Then Jacqueline rose to the occasion, greeting her guest with cool charm. In a short time the lieutenant had become what is commonly known as the life of the party. He sang, he strummed Andy's guitar, he made jokes with José, and he discussed the smuggling of antiquities with Scoville. By midnight the party was in full swing, and everyone seemed to be having a fine time.

Jean was not. She had been suspicious of the party from the first, and di Cavallo's appearance confirmed her suspicions. He looked magnificent in his sweeping white toga, but Jean knew he was miscast. Mark Antony, the rough, tough soldier who had let passion for a woman override ambition, was not the right role for this man. Again Jean was reminded of the cold, handsome face which appears on so many statues in Rome: Augustus, the most enigmatic of all the Julians, a man ruled throughout his life by calculating intelligence.

It was exactly midnight when di Cavallo pounded on the table and proposed a toast. The hilarity was at its height and it took him several minutes to get them all together, with their glasses of wine. José's headdress was tipped onto the back of his head and Ted's moustache had run into a shapeless smudge. Scoville was sulking; he had been trying all evening without success to get Jacqueline out onto the balcony. Now they all gathered around the big table in the dining area of the *salone,* and di Cavallo opened a fresh bottle.

"A toast to a lovely and charming lady," he said, lifting his glass. "Our hostess."

They drank. Di Cavallo filled the glasses again.

"We thank her," he said oratorically, "for a memorable evening. For this masquerade. And now, my friends, the masquerade is almost over."

The change in his voice struck them, even Scoville, who had consumed more wine than anyone else. One by one the relaxed figures straightened and turned, until they sat like a circle of frozen images, staring at the man who stood at the head of the table.

"The masquerade is over," di Cavallo repeated The resemblance Jean had noticed was pronounced; the face was cold and beautiful and quite merciless. "Some of you, perhaps, have been deceived as to the purpose of this evening's entertainment. Yet I think that in your hearts none of you has ever been wholly deceived. You have known the truth, and tried for a number of different reasons to conceal it even from yourselves. But the truth cannot be concealed. It is time for it to emerge. It is time now."

Di Cavallo was enjoying himself. His expression had not lost any of its cool calm, but Jean sensed the streak of sadism underneath. His voice rolled.

"To come here under false pretenses was not the act of a gentleman. I feel no shame; because in my humble fashion I serve justice, and justice, my friends, sometimes demands the sacrifice of honor. Yet I cannot claim the credit for discovering the truth. That distinction rests with another, and it is for her to explain it to you."

His outstretched hand indicated Jacqueline. Gathering up the folds of his skirt in a royal gesture, he sat down.

Jacqueline's hands were loosely clasped around the stem of her glass and her eyes were fixed on the glowing burgundy liquid. She was as white as her robe, but her voice was perfectly steady when she began to speak.

"The lieutenant gives me too much credit—if that is the word. But I won't talk about blame or credit, honor or justice. This had to be done. Whether I like it or not is beside the point. In every human society, every culture of which we have record, one crime is the ultimate crime, punishable by the extreme penalty. On that, human ethics are unanimous. Murder is wrong."

She looked up. She was still pale, but her face had a shadow of the same ruthlessness Jean had seen in di Cavallo's. There was a stir around the silent table, a shift of bodies; but no sound.

"Albert's death was murder," Jacqueline went on. "I wonder how many of you were really deluded into thinking it anything else? The police were not. The scene was skillfully set, and at first the pattern seemed plain. But Lieutenant di Cavallo is far too good a policeman to be fooled. His intuition told him the truth, but there seemed no way of proving it, nor any way of finding the killer. It could be any one of a number of people. Yet the lieutenant was convinced that it was indeed one of that number. He supported the theory of suicide only because it seemed advantageous to let the killer think he had succeeded in that aspect of his crime."

She looked at Jean, and now there was a hint of apology in her voice.

"I went to the police, Jean, as soon as I realized you were in danger. It would have been inexcusable to do anything else. I expected to be laughed at, but that didn't bother me; ridicule, as a weapon, is only effective against the young. I was astounded to find the lieutenant was ready to believe me. Since then we have been working together. It has been a genuine collaboration; without the facts I was able to supply he could not have proceeded, but without him I would have been helpless to act."

She transferred her glance back to the tabletop, and her voice became impersonal again.

"We speculated about motive. The police were able to investigate the backgrounds of the suspects much more efficiently than I could, and they came up with some surprising facts." There was another uncomfortable stir around the table; Jacqueline disregarded it and went on.

"Though several of your case histories provided possible motives, no single suspicious fact emerged. It became clear to us that an inquiry into motive was a dead end. We had to go at the problem from another angle.

"Let us look, then, at the simple physical facts. Albert's death was carefully planned. Nothing contradicted an assumption of suicide. Even if one assumed it was a case of murder, no clue indicated one suspect over another. It might be argued that a woman could not commit such a crime. By its very nature it would seem to demand physical strength and a certain degree of ruthlessness. But the modern female is not the fragile vessel her ancestress was. For all his bulk, Albert was not particularly muscular. And it wasn't difficult to imagine circumstances in which a woman might have found it easier than a man to get Albert into a vulnerable position. On his knees, perhaps, her hand twining in his hair as she bent over him. . . . It isn't a pleasant picture, I agree; but very little about this case was pleasant.

"The question of alibis is inconclusive. At least three of you were in the lowest level, not far from the scene of the crime, within minutes of its discovery. I include Jean, of course. To the police she was as prominent a suspect as anyone else. And she mentioned having spoken to Michael and to Dana just before she found Albert. None of the others has verifiable alibis, except for Ted and Ann. According to the priest on duty, they were talking to him at the time the murder was discovered. The only flaw in this alibi is that we are not sure how long Albert lay there before being found. I thought, then, that it was unlikely he could have lingered for very long, but I am told by the police surgeon that there are some amazing examples of survival. So, although I was inclined to eliminate Ted and Ann, I could not do so completely."

So far none of this was new to Jean; but she was sickly amused to note that the tactful first person plural with which Jacqueline had begun had now become an unequivocal "I."

"Thanks to your restless habits," Jacqueline continued, "I couldn't give anyone an alibi for the other suspicious events. Jean had two so-called "accidents" before the incident in the pool, when she nearly drowned. All three attacks were carefully planned; any one of them might have been accepted as the accident it appeared to be. The first one, caused by a toy left on the darkened stairs of her apartment building, was a most oblique type of attack; there was absolutely no way of tracing it back to its perpetrator. By that very fact, it was also inherently unsuccessful. I regard it as a wild stroke; something that might or might not work, but which was worth a try because it involved so little risk to the killer.

"The second attempt was more direct—pushing Jean into the path of a car. Here, one would think, the murderer took a greater risk. And yet again it was impossible to alibi any of you. The time of day was well chosen; it was the lunch-siesta period, when the streets are crowded. It is true that you are all rather distinctive-looking, easily recognized. But wigs are cheap here; a change of clothing, or simple disguise, could make any of you safe from a casual glance. And that incident had its own built-in safeguards. If Jean had recognized a friend she would have hailed him—or her—and then the attempt would not have been made. After she had fallen into the street, the chance of her being able to recognize anyone was, to say the least, unlikely.

"The third attempt took place here, in the pool; and I find it hard to forgive myself for that, because I was expecting it. Expecting—and praying that it wouldn't happen. It did happen, right under my nose, and only luck got her out alive that time. And again I found it impossible to clear any of the suspects. But the incident confirmed what had been until then only a nasty hunch.

"The attempt in the pool also demonstrated the killer was getting desperate. The more 'accidents' Jean had, the less plausible they became; and in the third case the killer had to take an extraordinary risk of being recognized. I could only conclude that his need to silence Jean was great. She must pose a threat so potentially dangerous that he had to risk drawing official attention back to this little circle of people—the Seven Sinners, as Andy calls them."

"One moment," Scoville said. "May I point out one flaw in your masterful exposition? You claim the murderer had to silence Jean because of her knowledge. What if he is that strange but not uncommon type, a killer who enjoys killing? Could not these crimes have been committed by an outsider who hates students, or foreigners, or something of the sort?"

Jacqueline nodded. Jean noticed that she would not meet Scoville's eyes.

"I considered the possibility, of course. However, the police eliminated the tourists who were in the church when Albert died. On that occasion, and again in the third attempt on Jean's life, the only people present were the students. Add the fact that Jean was the one to find Albert, the one to whom he tried to speak, and I think you will admit the conclusion is hard to avoid."

She waited, courteously. Scoville shrugged, and leaned back in his chair.

"Therefore," Jacqueline resumed, "I returned to the one fact that set Jean apart. Albert could not speak to her, but he did communicate. He scratched a symbol in the dust before he died. No one else saw it. It may have been purposely obliterated. More likely, it was wiped out when Albert fell forward in his death agony. But Jean was the only one to see it."

"So she says," Dana interrupted. Her voice was openly hostile.

"So she says," Jacqueline repeated. "Naturally one has to consider the possibility that Jean lied. But why should she? There have been murderers who thrust themselves into public view, either from arrogance or from an anxious desire to be on the scene and know what's happening. It is a stupid thing to do; the sensible killer lets someone else find the body and stays as quiet as he can. But let us assume Jean is this psychological type. Surely it would be foolish of her, though, to insist on facts that raised further suspicion and obscured the very impression she was trying to create. For the murderer obviously tried to suggest a case of suicide. If Jean was the killer and wished to invent a last message from her victim, wouldn't she invent one that strengthened the assumption of suicide?

"I was forced, then, to the conclusion that Jean's story was true. But what a confusing story it was! Not only did Albert's message make no sense, but Jean had told it to everyone in the group, including the police. I kept coming up against that, like a brick wall; there seemed to be no point in trying to silence her after she had spoken.

"But was that single symbol the full extent of Albert's message? Perhaps Jean had not told all she knew."

"I did," Jean interrupted. "I keep telling you—"

"So you did. And I believed it. Let us suppose, however, that he wrote something other than what you say he wrote. The only possible reason you might have for concealing the truth was if Albert had written something which betrayed the identity of the killer. You might lie if he had accused you—or someone you cared for deeply enough to lie for him.

"That was feasible—before I started examining it. For, then, all you had to do was keep silent. Albert was dead when I arrived; you had time to obliterate his scrawl and claim you had found him dead. No one would have questioned such a statement; the police surgeon was astounded that he had lived so long. Every hypothesis seemed to lead me back to the same conclusion: that you had told the literal truth. The very meaninglessness of the statement made it more believable. For why should you invent a message that made no sense?

"I thought," said Jacqueline wryly, "I was going to burst a blood vessel in my brain over that crazy seven. I went through every wild theory I could think of. I pursued saints, because I was haunted by Albert's *idée fixe.* He had been obsessed by his saints, and I became obsessed too. Nothing came of it; not, at least, in the way I expected.

"The revelation finally came that day in the catacombs. Looking at the numbers over the lintel of the tomb, it hit me like a thunderbolt. Jean had never written the number, she had only named it. I scared her to death, and made the rest of you think I was losing my wits, by demanding she write it out. And, as I had come to expect, it was the Roman numeral instead of our familiar, Arabic seven.

"Up to that point, my confusion had been open, and openly expressed. After that . . ." Jacqueline's voice changed, and Jean felt her muscles tighten. This was it. They were getting to it now.

"I acted," Jacqueline admitted. Her pallor was more pronounced. "I still didn't have any proof, and I was afraid of what the killer might do next. I was no longer concerned for Jean, for I felt sure she had now expressed the knowledge the killer had tried to keep her from telling. It must have been a hideous shock to him when he learned Albert had lived long enough to leave an abortive but damning message. He saw its significance at once; but he was clever enough to realize that the significance might be obscured forever if he could keep Jean from repairing her inadvertent blunder."

Jacqueline took a sip of wine, and put the glass down. The wine, or some more subtle intoxicant, had stiffened her resolve. There were bright spots of color in her cheeks, and her eyes were angry.

"Sevens," she said. "Sevens all over the scene—scattered, like chaff, to confuse the picture. I said once, remember, that you were all overeducated. Didn't any of you see the truth, even after reading the inscription on the tomb? Was it too obvious for the subtle academic brain, or was the killer too successful in obscuring the issue? Yet he wasn't the only one; we all did it. I did it myself. And all the while the simple, obvious explanation was staring us in the face."

She looked around the circle, and the others looked back, unspeaking, almost unbreathing. Jacqueline banged her hand down on the table, and they all jumped; the wine glass tipped, spilling a small puddle of red onto the smooth mahogany.

"What would a dying man choose for his last message?" Jacqueline demanded. "Forget the subtleties and the ingenious theories. I've read the classic thrillers myself, and I know all the variations. I've admired the ingenuity of the author even while I questioned his basic premise. Because a dying man is not at his keenest intellectually, I question whether he could go through the tortuous deductions that mystery writers attribute to him, in order to produce a cleverly confusing message. And don't bring up that brilliant but equally unconvincing variant—that a dying man might produce a deliberately ambiguous message because his murderer is still present. Obviously the murderer would destroy anything he wrote. What does a dying man want to tell the world?"

Again her eyes went around the circle. Di Cavallo, who presumably knew the answer, was silent. He was smiling very slightly, but the upward curve of his lips did not warm his expression. Finally—of all people—Michael answered.

"The name of the person who killed him," he said.

"Yes," Jacqueline said. "And that is what Albert tried to write."

"Seven?" Ted said. "I still don't—"

"You're still bemused by the number. Hypnotized, as

we all were. Forget the number. It has nothing to do with it. Albert didn't write a number. Look," Jacqueline said, with a terrible weariness. "This is what he wrote."

She used the puddle of wine for ink, so the word came out crudely scrawled with the tip of a reddened finger, as the dying man might have written it.

VII.

Someone got it. There was an intake of breath, so sharp it must have hurt the throat that made it. Jean didn't look up to see who had reacted. Her eyes were glued to the red letters.

"And this," said Jacqueline, "is what he was trying to write."

Her finger dipped again into the crimson puddle.

VIRGINIA.

Scoville pushed his chair back. It screamed like a living creature across the marble floor.

"Prove it," he said. "There are so many possible variations—"

"Not all that many," Jacqueline said. "The third letter, which Albert never completed, might be any one of a number of letters—*E, L, P, B*—others. But starting from this, the rest of the case can be, and has been, built up. The motive only made sense after we knew who the murderer was. And there is only one person in this group whose name begins with those three—or two and a half—letters."

Jean knew then. But she still didn't believe it.

"You're all accustomed to nicknames," Jacqueline said. "Albert wasn't, though. The first day I met him he insisted on knowing my correct name and title. He had no sense of humor; the joke behind some of your epithets must have eluded him completely. All this is irrelevant, really. What matters is that even before I checked the official records I was able to deduce which of you had a given name that matched Albert's scrawl."

For the first time since the talk had begun she looked directly at the two people sitting across the table from her. They always looked a great deal alike; now, in their common horror, the resemblance of their features was uncanny.

"Raggedy Ann and Andy," she said. "I'm an old-fashioned librarian, you know. As soon as I saw the hair and heard the names I remembered the stories. They were charming characters, those two rag dolls; but I wondered whether parents would really christen their children with those names—particularly when the son and daughter were born a year apart. I noticed that sometimes people called one of you Ginger. That's a logical nickname for a redhead; it becomes even more logical when the given name is Virginia—Ginnie—you see? I noted also that the other was sometimes called junior. This can be a term of affection, but it is often a literal designation. Those are your real names, aren't they? Samuel Junior and Virginia. Albert knew both of you when you were children. He would think of you by the names he used then—not by family nicknames, which would not have been employed by your teachers."

"No," Andy said suddenly. "I'm not going to let you get away with this. Of course you're right about the names; when have we ever made a mystery of them? They're on all the records, passports. . . . We've used the nicknames for years. All you've done is cook up a crazy theory on the basis of a wild coincidence. You try it in court! Go ahead! That alibi of Annie's is better than you think."

"I agree," Jacqueline said.

Scoville sat up in his chair. Andy, stopped in mid-peroration, stared stupidly. Jacqueline said wearily,

"Of course all this is worthless legally. But the motive isn't."

"What motive? What reason could anyone have—"

"We go back," said Jacqueline, "to the saints. They kept cropping up, didn't they? There was one fact, at the very beginning, that would have made me wonder about the theory of suicide even if Jean hadn't started having accidents. When the police searched Albert's room, they found only a pitiable scrawl which presumably represented his total output after a year or more of work. It was incoherent and rambling—the product of a sick mind.

"We've all agreed that Albert was peculiar. But mental illness is not a discrete disease with a single set of symptoms, like chicken pox. I questioned—as did Jean— whether Albert's eccentricities were those of a man who might develop suicidal tendencies. Never once did he indicate any doubt of the value of his work. Fanatics of that type don't kill themselves. They cannot be convinced of the worthlessness of their life's work, because their belief in it is not based on rational premises. Up till the end Albert was enthusiastic, cocksure, contemptuous of critics.

"These attributes characterize the screwballs who hang around the lunatic fringes of scholarship. But they are also characteristic of scholars who are regarded as fanatics by their contemporaries. Classical scholars jeered at Schliemann and his dreams of Troy. Galileo and Semmelweis fought all their lives for recognition. I needn't go on; there are many examples.

"The fact that Albert had an *idée fixe* did not prove his idea was wrong. If he wasn't mad, if he didn't commit suicide—then what of his behavior on the night of the party? Was it possible that his wild accusation was not a sign of paranoia, but a statement of fact? Was this, in short, a crime for gain?

"We theorized about a family heirloom, a genuine treasure, which could have been possessed by a man who was grindingly poor in every other way. And all the while the answer was staring us in the face. Albert did own one thing of supreme value to him—his treasure. His work, in other words.

"To my surprise, I found a single assumption answered all my questions. It explained Albert's accusation and the discrepancy between the scanty sheaf of papers found in his room and the bulging briefcase he carried—a briefcase so heavy it made him walk lopsided. It also provided a motive for murder. If Albert had stumbled on something important, a discovery worth stealing, it could not be stolen with impunity. Albert was not stupid; if another scholar had published his discovery he would have recognized it. And while he might not have been able to prove it was originally his, he could raise enough fuss to seriously discredit the thief. Scholarly reputations are fragile."

"But," Jean said, "I thought you said it was murder for gain. Doesn't that mean—"

"Killing to gain possession of something which is not rightfully yours. Our trouble is that we think in material terms. Yet you of all people—scholars and artists—should realize that there are desires much more compulsive than the desire for mere money. Someone needed an idea, a piece of original work. Good God, a man can earn money, or steal it in comparative safety these days; it is much less logical to kill for monetary gain than for an intangible which cannot be procured by such simple means. You've got it or you haven't got it, as the saying goes. The one thing a man cannot produce on demand is a genuine creative idea. And if he needs it badly enough . . ."

"You speak in riddles now," said José. "I admit your point; you are right, we can surely comprehend the hunger for scholarly fame. But you do not speak of Ann. She is a sculptor. She could not use the work of a man like Albert."

"That is true. Yet Albert thought his attacker was Ann."

"A disguise," Andy said sharply. "You spoke of that earlier—how easy it would be—"

Jacqueline broke in. "Yes, a disguise. Who? Most of you are automatically eliminated, if my theory of motive is correct. Michael is like Ann, he couldn't use Albert's discovery. Neither could José. Jean? Again, no. As a librarian, I know how narrow your scholarly fields are. Jean has been working in medieval art history. She couldn't produce a book on Paleo-Christian hagiology without raising eyebrows. That only leaves three possibilities. The three people who deal, in one form or another, with Roman archaeology and history. Because we can't be sure, even now, precisely what form Albert's work took."

Slowly, inevitably, all eyes focused on a single figure.

"No!" Dana exclaimed. Clumsily she got to her feet. The appeal of Cleopatra had fled; there was only a sallow, rather chubby girl in a funny costume, fumbling at the table to keep from falling. "No, I didn't! I couldn't! I—"

"Someone catch her," Jacqueline said "She's going to fall. She didn't do it."

"She's a girl," Andy said. "The only one who could disguise herself as Ann. A wig—"

"Don't you see," Jacqueline interrupted, "that it's no use, Andy? You can't use Albert's material now. It would be a dead giveaway, after this. You've failed; it was all for nothing. Won't you speak, and end this? It's too hard on— on everyone."

Andy shook his head.

"You're crazy," he said in a low voice. "A crazy old—"

Jacqueline glanced at Scoville. She spoke quickly, as if she wanted to get it over as quickly as possible.

"The light in the murder room was poor, but it was not that poor. Dana couldn't by any conceivable trick have made Albert think she was Ann. Their figures, for one thing . . . And clothing; the killer didn't have time for elaborate changes of costume, nor could he walk into the church carrying a suitcase. Even a wig would require a box. Ted is the only other person who might have had a motive, and I needn't point out the absurdity of his trying to disguise himself. But the resemblance between Ann and her brother is striking. Ann is tall for a girl and Albert was short; he wouldn't have noticed the height differential unless brother and sister were together. Hair, clothing—they were both wearing dark slacks and shirt that day—all Andy needed was a smear of lipstick, a scarf over his head, and a pair of sunglasses. It would serve, for long enough to do the job.

"Once I knew the truth, everything pointed to Andy. He fits both criteria—motive and means—and he is the only one who does. It would be natural for Albert to talk to Andy about his work; Albert thought of him as a boyhood friend and a fellow enthusiast. Albert's English was poor, and his conversation was hard to follow; but Andy knows French and, I suspect, more Arabic than he admits. He's an excellent linguist. He is the one among you most likely to understand what Albert was doing, and to recognize a meaningful discovery. He is also the one who could most easily profit from Albert's work. It is, essentially, his own field. And he needs an idea. Shortly the trustees will be deciding on the renewal of the fellowships. Andy must have his. Everyone expects him to get it. And he is . . . Sam, I'm sorry; I'm not blaming you, no one could; but he is haunted by the fear of failing, failing himself and you. A different kind of child might have reacted differently to the magnificent image you project. Andy felt impelled to equal and surpass it."

"My thesis," Andy said in a strange, high voice. "I don't need to steal ideas from anybody. He's brilliant, Andy is. He's brighter than anybody in the whole—"

"Oh, God," Dana muttered.

"The thesis," Jacqueline said. "And the boy, the friend,

who committed suicide. Who had the nervous break-down, Andy? How often has Ann lied to protect you? Did she know, in that other case, or did she only suspect?"

Andy fought visibly for control. The wild light in his eyes faded, and his quivering features grew hard.

"Now stop it," he said. His voice was so calm, so reasonable that they all stirred uneasily. "I'll end this business right now. You're saying the murderer is the one who stole Albert's work, right? Albert claimed his precious whatever-it-was was stolen the day of the party—when he went out to eat. All right. I was in the library that afternoon, the whole bloody time. Some of you must have seen me there."

"He is right," Ted said. "I was in the stacks at noon, and saw him in his office. For several hours thereafter I sat in the reading room. I would have seen him if he had left."

"I saw him too," Jean said.

"All right," Jacqueline said. "To the last painful word, is that it? Ann."

Ann had been sitting with her grotesquely painted face hidden in her hands. She looked up. Tears had streaked the makeup, but her face did not look at all comic.

"One or the other of you is going to be accused of murder," Jacqueline said. "The logic can't be faulted. The motive can be applied to either; your devotion to your brother is well known, you might steal for him. You would probably prefer suffering yourself to seeing him suffer. You've done it all your life. But can you let him go free, knowing him for what he is? He's sick; he may not be incurable. Whether he is or not, whether or not you are ready to sacrifice yourself for him, you have no moral right to sacrifice his potential victims. This will happen again."

For a long moment the whole room waited, without breathing. Then Ann's head drooped.

"It was me," she said, so softly they had to strain to hear. "In the library that day. You said—how easy it is for us to look like each other. . . . He said it was part of a practical joke. Then, after Albert died . . . Nobody ever asked! And I didn't want to believe . . ."

Di Cavallo had been poised and ready, but Andy's supple quickness caught him off guard. It was Michael who pulled the clawed fingers from Ann's throat, and it took both of them to hold him until he finally collapsed into a sobbing heap. But bad as it was, Jean knew this was not the sight that would haunt her. It was Scoville's face, as he cursed his daughter for betraying his son.

TEN

TOWARD morning a thunderstorm moved in over the city, in a spectacular display of Jovian thunder and lightning. Next day the air over Rome was sparklingly clear. The mighty dome of Michelangelo floated on a sea of green branches. The suburban streets looked as if they had been newly painted in the warm earth colors Jean would always remember when she thought of Rome—umber and orange, gold and brick-red. The sky had the heavenly blue shade Fra Angelico used in the cloaks of his Madonnas, and wild poppies glowed like rubies in an empty lot beside the café.

Jean was the only customer at Gino's. She had left the apartment early that morning, before Jacqueline awoke, and she didn't expect any of the others to join her in their old haunt. The Seven Sinners would never meet again; and the commonplace neighborhood café held memories she would not be able to face comfortably for a time.

Yet when she recognized the two figures coming up the hill she was, somehow, not surprised. At the sight of them something shifted and fell back into focus. The past could not be obliterated; it had to be endured. And among its memories were some that were too good to be discarded.

José was back in his customary suits of solemn black, but the ghost of Montezuma still haunted his aquiline face. Ted looked the same, outwardly, but there was something different about his expression, and a new swing to his step. They greeted her rather diffidently.

"We hoped you would come," Ted said. "But we wondered—"

"About many things," José interrupted. "We could hardly linger, last night, to ask questions."

"Don't expect any answers from me," Jean said. "I'm just as baffled as you are. The whole thing—"

Her voice broke. José said calmly,

"Was unendurable. That is why we must ask the questions, talk like little gossips. It is the only way—to extract the commonplace and the rational from disaster. It could have been worse." Meeting Jean's eyes, he added, "You might have loved him. That would have been worse."

"I did love him. The same way I love all of you."

Ted nodded.

"Our feelings for one another run deeper than I had realized. But you must admit there is a difference between those feelings and the one José is talking about."

"Yes. For a while I thought . . . Hey, look! Isn't that Jacqueline?"

"Jacqueline and Michael," José corroborated.

Michael was looking almost spruce this morning; not only had he shaved, he had combed his hair and he wore his "good" shirt—the one without holes. Jacqueline was faultlessly attired in a blue linen suit. Her purse and gloves were of the same pale ivory as her shoes, and her hair was coiled into a knot at the back of her neck.

The two men rose to honor this sartorial elegance, and José pulled out a chair.

"I expected you," he said.

"I had to come." Pulling off her gloves, Jacqueline looked at each of them in turn. "I'm leaving Rome today, and I may not see you again.

"But I knew you'd all be bursting with questions. I owe you that much, to know the truth before it comes out in the newspapers."

Now that the invitation had been given, none of them could think of anything to say. After a moment Jacqueline said, with a faint smile,

"I wasn't sure any of you would be speaking to me."

"Why not?" Ted asked in astonishment. "Oh! Oh, I see. You are thinking of the stool-pigeon syndrome, perhaps. We are not a street gang, to place loyalty to the mob above all other virtues."

"You yourself said it," José added. "In all cultures there is one ultimate crime."

"Not to mention the minor detail of Jean's skin being

kept intact," Michael contributed. "We like it in the shape it's in."

"Sorry," Jacqueline said ruefully. "I guess I've been dealing with the less logical segment of your age group for too long."

"Before we start asking questions," Ted said, "maybe we should wait to see if Dana is coming."

"She's coming," Jacqueline said. An odd little smile curved her mouth. "But we needn't wait. . . . Ah, here she is."

A car came down the street. It was not until it pulled over to the curb and parked, in bland disregard of the sign forbidding such activity, that they recognized the occupants. The vehicle was an open sports car, silver in color, and di Cavallo was at the wheel. Beside him, Dana looked as smug as a Persian cat.

The two got out of the car and joined the others. After greetings had been exchanged, di Cavallo said briskly,

"Have you finished your lecture, then?"

"I haven't even begun. Really, I think we covered most everything last night, didn't we?"

"One thing I did not understand," José said. "The reference to an earlier suicide—a friend of Andy's. Was that really as it sounded to me?"

"It was one of the facts that turned up in the police investigation of your backgrounds," Jacqueline said, after waiting for a moment to see whether di Cavallo would answer. "However, there had been references to it more than once. Nothing can be proved now; there is no need, it would only cause needless pain for the boy's parents. But I think—I am almost sure—it was Andy's first venture into murder. His much-admired thesis was written after his friend died."

"I don't see how Andy could get away with it," Jean said. "What about the boy's adviser, his other friends? Wasn't anyone suspicious?"

"How much do you know of the details of anyone else's work? It's amazing how seldom people really listen to one another. The boy's adviser? Well, believe it or not, I wrote a thesis once myself in the prehistoric past. I met my adviser once a month, and he told me the latest cute stories about his dog. Maybe that's an exaggeration, but the amount of genuine communication between us was very limited. At least he was willing to meet with me. Not all advisers are."

"Master's or doctor's dissertation?" José asked.

"What's your field?" Ted demanded.

"That's beside the point," Jacqueline said demurely. "I am merely trying to demonstrate that Andy was fairly safe in stealing someone else's ideas. Assume the unlikely did occur and someone noted a resemblance between his work and the tentative theories of another man. The conclusion would be that the other man had copied Andy. No, there was very little risk for Andy. If he hadn't panicked and attacked Jean, he might have gotten away with Albert's murder."

"Except for the detective talents of Mrs. Kirby," said Ted. "To what do you attribute your success?"

"To a unique combination of circumstances that could never possibly recur," Jacqueline said, rather too forcefully. "A librarian is a hanger-on around the fringes of the scholarly world. I knew enough about that world to comprehend the motive, but not enough to get bogged down in the irrelevant details that confused the rest of you. And if there's one thing we learn in my job, it's research. We deal with many fields; we don't know much about any one of them, but we do know where to go to get the facts. I know, there are some librarians who regard books as little boxes to be arranged and classified and rebound from time to time; but you'd be surprised how many of us actually read the darned things! I started out in a small town library, where I covered a little of everything from children's books to archaeology and mystery stories. I've read hundreds of thrillers, and I've always been skeptical of those complicated dying messages."

"Me, too," Michael said. He was doodling again; he didn't even look up from his sketch pad.

Jacqueline stared at him.

"Are you trying to tell me—"

"Oh, sure, I saw that part of it right away." Michael looked up and smiled angelically. "I don't think in Roman numerals either."

"After all my pompous remarks . . . Why didn't you say something?"

"What, for instance? People think I'm crazy anyhow, especially the fuzz—er, police. I didn't know about Albert's work, or any of that jazz, remember. I just thought maybe he cornered Annie and she flipped. I always liked Annie."

There was a baffled silence. Then di Cavallo said, in a muted roar, "Young man. Am I to understand—"

"I couldn't fit Jean's accidents into it, though," Michael went on calmly. "I didn't think Annie would hurt Jean, but

. . . I didn't know what to think."

"You thought about Andy," Jacqueline said.

"Yeah, sure. After Albert accused him of stealing his precious. Shades of Tolkien . . . Albert was definitely a Gollum type, you know." The silence got to him after a while. He looked up, saw the circle of fascinated faces, and blushed slightly. "Well, why else would Albert come straight to the Scovilles' apartment after he found his treasure was missing? Nobody told him about the party; we didn't want him horning in. It had to be Ann or Andy he was looking for. I don't know much French, but that was a masculine noun he used—"

" '*Voleur!*' " Jean exclaimed. "How could we have been so dumb?"

"And," Michael went on, "the way Andy moved in on him, to shut him up before he could say too much, was very cool. Andy can—could—talk the leg off a table; I suppose he told Albert some story, promised to help him track down the thief, or said he'd borrowed the material, or something. . . . Andy ducked out, then, into the john, and not long afterwards Albert passed out. It was too quick and neat to be coincidental. Ann mentioned once they had sleeping pills. Even so, I couldn't be sure about Andy. I thought of Albert's treasure as some family jewel or other, couldn't dig why Andy would want a thing like that."

Jacqueline opened her purse and took out a sheet of paper.

"Michael says I can keep this, Jean. Is that okay with you?"

"Sure," Jean said, recognizing the line of saints. The

sketch of Andy, debonair as Saint George, made her feel a little sick.

"This," said Jacqueline, spreading it out, "was a graphic statement of the truth. It hit me with quite a shock when I saw it."

They studied it in absorbed silence; most of them had not seen it before.

"Who the hell . . . oh," Dana said. "Mary Magdalene. Michael, I don't think I like that look. . . ."

"Nor do I," José said. "One of these days, Michael, someone is going to send you a bomb through the mail."

"It may be me," Ted said. "Saint Stephen indeed. I admit that it may have a certain appropriateness—perhaps more than you realize."

"Oh, I realize," Michael said. "I know who your new girl friend is. Talk about martyr complexes . . . If your old man doesn't kill you, she will."

"So everyone knows," Ted said resignedly. "Except my father . . . He soon will. I wrote to him this morning."

"I don't know," Dana said. "Have you jilted your fiancée? Men are all finks."

"That other was a family affair," Ted said defensively. "She will not be hurt; she didn't care."

"Yeah," Michael said, "but to get involved with an Arab girl . . ."

"Not only an Arab," Ted said. "She is a member of a Palestinian guerrilla group."

There was a short, respectful silence. Remembering the handsome hawk face of the girl in the café, Jean understood. Apparently Michael had gone through some of his student contacts to discover the girl's identity.

"But surely," said di Cavallo, as intrigued as the others, "isn't that a trifle . . . ?"

"Not a trifle. My father will disown me," Ted said. His voice was resigned, but there was a light in his eyes that made him look even more like Michael's sketch. "But feelings do not follow politics, do they? And not all of us, in my generation, are so free of guilt as our fathers, with their one obsession. To repossess Eretz Israel, we dispossessed half a million people. Do the sufferings of millions of Jews, through thousands of years, justify the infliction of more suffering, on others? Since I fought in the war my feelings have changed. I have argued with my father; now I argue with Salwa, because I do not believe that her kind of violence will right this new wrong any more than our violence against her people righted our ancient wrong. I hope to convert her—not to change her principles, but her methods. Someday, out of all this, there must be a way to peace."

"Ishmael and Isaac were both sons of Abraham," Jacqueline murmured. "I admire your principles, Ted. I hope you succeed. But the moderate usually gets stoned by both sides."

"I have methods of persuasion with Salwa which are quite effective," Ted said modestly. "If I go down under the stones I will go down fighting. And," he added with a sudden grin, "I shall have one hell of a good time before I fall."

"And we thought you were a spy," Jean said. The look on Ted's face made her laugh. "You wouldn't believe some of the things we thought. I didn't suspect Andy any more than I did the rest of you."

"Michael did," Jacqueline said. She pointed to the sketch. "His identifications were—forgive me, Dana—alarmingly accurate. All his saints were pacifists except one. Saint George was the heroic murderer, the only one of the lot who committed violence. And he was the patron of the Crusaders. They did a lot of damage among the Arabs, if you recall."

"I wasn't thinking of that," Michael muttered.

"That's what makes you so terrifying," Jacqueline said severely. "You don't think; you just reach in and drag out people's souls. Why did you make Ann into Saint Barbara?"

"Needed some virgin saint or other."

"Yet her legend is very suggestive. It was her father, if you recall, who locked her in the tower, and later betrayed her."

"Which stood out like a billboard." Michael's voice was savage. "Damn that bastard Scoville; he's the one who caused all this."

"Don't dump on my generation," Jacqueline said. "We're the victims of our genes and our surroundings and our parents, just as you are."

"Blame is useless," José said heavily. "We are all victims. . . . And I feel myself particularly a victim. I should rather be Beelzebub than Saint Augustine, as you show him."

"I don't get it," Dana said, staring blankly at the sketch. "None of them make any sense, except maybe Jean as a little lamb. . . . And this one of Jake is downright blasphemous."

"Not blasphemous, just plain insulting," Jacqueline

said. "I may be a reluctant mother, Michael, but my halo is not a bit ragged. It's big and shiny and neat, and I earned it over twenty-one hard-working years."

Michael smiled.

"Talk about hangups," he said. "You didn't want to get involved with us, did you? It was a case of the triumph of instinct over common sense."

"Not instinct—habit. In both my professional capacities I've been laying down the law to the young for twenty years." Jacqueline rose, picking up her purse. "So now I think I'm entitled to a weekend off. If I don't see you again, I'll be following your varied careers with considerable interest. In my reluctant way, I've become rather fond of all of you."

Di Cavallo was on his feet; the others followed suit, even the girls. The occasion seemed to demand something, but no one knew exactly what to say. It was José who found the words.

"Be of good cheer," he said, his dark eyes intent on the older woman's face. "No man is immortal."

The ancient pagan epitaph should have sounded strange from him, as he stood straight and tall in the dark robe of the militant Christian order, but it seemed to strike the right note. Jacqueline's sober face relaxed into a smile.

"Good-bye," she said.

Di Cavallo followed her as she walked swiftly to the car. He opened the door for her, and closed it; then, with one sweep of his long legs, he got into the driver's seat and started the engine. It was not until the car had pulled away; with a triumphant roar of the exhaust, that the abandoned watchers fully grasped what had happened. Jean looked from one blank face to the next. Dana's expression put the final touch on the situation. Jean burst into shouts of laughter.

"Outfought and outmaneuvered," she gasped. "Sorry, Dana; I can't help it."

"I wonder where they are going," Ted said.

"None of our business. Do you realize how little we know about that lady? Did she ever a mention a husband?"

"If she did, this is not the time to bring it up," José said.

Dana's face was still a study. Finally her mouth relaxed into a grudging smile.

"That son of a gun," she said, using a more explicit term. "He's been rushing me like crazy the last few days. And all he wanted was an excuse to be on the spot at the right moment."

"Maybe he was protecting you," Michael said coolly. "Didn't you ever think you might be in danger?"

Dana paled

"You're trying to scare me."

"I've been thinking some more," Michael said pensively. "Everybody, including Andy, thought Jean was his big danger. I'm not so sure. The fuzz aren't Latinists, and they have those nice simple minds like Jake keeps bragging about; so they would have been on the track, probably, if they had ever seen the seven written out. Di Cavallo must have known the official names, since he checked us out with the Embassy and all that. But I don't see how he could have proved anything. That's why they had to stage that sticky little drama last night. Without a confession—"

"All right, all right," Dana said impatiently. "What about me?"

"The seven clue was useless without the motive," Michael went on, maddeningly deliberate. "So long as Albert was considered a crackpot there was no way of nailing Andy for the murder. Which reminds me—there's a question nobody asked. At some point Andy substituted his crazy composition for Albert's real notes. But the big question is—how could he steal the material and risk leaving Albert on the loose? He must have known the guy would complain."

Dana, still morosely wrestling with the unpalatable possibility Michael had presented, was silent. It was Ted who asked meekly,

"All right, Holmes. How?"

"I'm not even Watson," Michael said. "But Jake and I were talking about it on the way up here. We'll never know for sure, unless Andy . . . But Jake thinks Andy tried to knock Albert out earlier—left him a drink loaded with dope or something. Obviously it didn't work. But the technique is typical of Andy; he tried the indirect method at first, with Jean, before he closed in on her."

Dana took a deep breath.

"What about me?" she cried. "You said—"

"I'm getting to that. Now, as I said, it was unlikely that di Cavallo would ever figure out the motive. He isn't a scholar, and he accepted our evaluation of Albert. But there were two people who knew enough about Albert's subject to be able to spot the value of his work—you, Dana, and Ted. Ted is an Israeli, and a male—on both counts not the kind of audience Albert would seek out.

You, on the other hand . . ."

Dana's face was green.

"But I did know. I mean—didn't any of you—"

"Ah, no," José muttered. He smote himself heavily on the brow. "I do not believe this. You knew?"

"Well, yes. I mean—"

"You knew," Jose shouted, "that that miserable young fool was not a fool, that those pitiful notes were not his, that he had found a valuable and important thing—and you did not contradict the police when they talked of suicide?"

"Yes—no!" Dana was close to tears. "I never thought of it like that. . . . I mean, people kill themselves for weird reasons! How was I to know the notes weren't his? And that weird idea of his—it was just weird, I didn't know! He kept following me around, you know how he was, and he talked all the time, and I didn't pay much attention—"

"Now, now," Ted said soothingly. "We understand. No imagination," he explained sadly to the others. "Combined with a greatly inflated ego . . . What do you expect? As Jacqueline said, no one ever listens."

"He might have killed me," Dana sniffed.

"I doubt that you were in danger." José looked a little sheepish. "Dana, I apologize for shouting. You understand, it was prompted by frustrated curiosity. For days we have been talking about Albert's work, and his great discovery, and his treasure; and none of us knows what it is! Relieve our curiosity, since you are the only one who can."

"Well, I didn't really listen," Dana repeated. She blew her nose into the handkerchief José handed her; Gino's café did not boast such amenities as napkins. "It was something about a saint's tomb, under one of the churches."

The others exchanged glances. Ted said delicately, "Do you happen to remember which church?"

"No. Oh—Saint Petra, something like that."

"Could it have been Santa Petronilla?" José asked.

"Right, that was it. He'd been reading old manuscripts. You know, the *Notitia ecclesiarum* and ancient pilgrims' books—that stuff."

"Yes, I know that stuff," José said in an odd voice. "Pilgrims began coming to Rome even before the fourth century. They wrote travel books . . . an incurable habit. . . . Do you mean Albert stumbled upon a reference no one else ever noticed?"

"Not just one—it was, like, putting together a lot of clues from different sources. Like with St. Peter's. Wasn't there someone, back in the third century, who wrote that he saw Saint Peter's memorial on the Vatican? Nobody paid much attention to it until they dug and found the memorial. It was like that. Somebody saw the tomb, way back when, and said it had a long inscription on it. Something about the daughter of Saint Peter. I remember that because it struck me as weird. I didn't even know he was married."

"Married," José repeated, like a machine. "Inscription . . . But no. If such a thing once existed, it must have been destroyed. Albert was a crazy fanatic."

"Andy wasn't," Jean reminded them. "He valued Albert's work enough to steal it. You know—it isn't impossible. I bet Albert knew more about the virgin saints than anybody. Even his obsession gave him an advantage; he would take literally facts that other students might dismiss as legend."

"Like Schliemann and the *Iliad*," José agreed.

"He kept comparing himself with Schliemann," Dana said. "He had it all worked out. He even got down into the crypt of the church and found a fragment of stonework that matched someone's description back in 1143—oh, I don't know how he did it, but he was convinced the tomb was still there."

José kept shaking his head.

"It is more than possible," Ted said, his eyes glittering as the idea grew on him. "It has happened before. Several of the catacombs were lost during the Middle Ages and only rediscovered in modern times. What a fantastic thing!"

Dana was sniffling pathetically into José's handkerchief.

"Now stop it, all of you," Jean said. She leaned across the table and patted the other girl's hand. "Don't mind them, Dana. Michael was putting you on. Where's that darned Gino? We all need some coffee."

Gino stood in the doorway, wiping his hands on his apron. His eyes moved over the group and then, for the first time, he spoke to them as fellow human. beings.

"Where are the others? The young boy and the girl with the red hair. You are only five today, not seven."

"They won't be coming again," Michael said, in the painful silence. "But we'll be here, Gino. We'll all be here. For a little while longer."

Center Point Publishing
600 Brooks Road ● PO Box 1
Thorndike ME 04986-0001 USA

(207) 568-3717

US & Canada:
1 800 929-9108